PRAISE FOR
JAMES GORDON BENNETT'S
My Father's Geisha

"Don't miss this lyrical first novel about a family that holds itself
together more out of habit than anything else."
—*Seventeen*

"POIGNANT, FUNNY AND POWERFULLY PERCEP-
TIVE. . . . *MY FATHER'S GEISHA* is a string of gemlike
chapters forming a seamless novel of subtle character development
. . . [set in] the same culturally sterile, gung-ho world which Pat
Conroy so clearly described in *The Great Santini*. . . . It is a
tribute to the author to have pulled off the young, first-person
narration so successfully. . . . AN ACT OF CONSUMMATE
LITERARY SKILL. . . . PROFOUNDLY MOVING."
—*Washington Post Book World*

"CHARMING . . . POWERFUL, BEAUTIFULLY COM-
POSED. . . . Like a Chinese puzzle, it moves and changes,
revealing new, complex levels in every chapter. . . . EVERY-
THING YOU'D WANT IS HERE."
—*New Orleans Times-Picayune*

"A finely nuanced first novel. . . . Bennett demonstrates a
wonderful ear for dialogue and a storyteller's sure touch. . . .
MY FATHER'S GEISHA is a funny, perceptive, and painful look
at the difficulties of family relationships."
—*Publishers Weekly*

"*MY FATHER'S GEISHA* is a tale of the demise of a family unit
amidst the military call for order. JAMES GORDON BEN-
NETT'S CLEAR AND PRECISE LANGUAGE, HIS STONE-
SOBER VISION, MAKE THIS A FUNNY AND HAUNTING
AND BEAUTIFUL BOOK."
—Bret Lott,
author of *The Man Who Owned Vermont*
and *A Dream of Old Leaves*

MY
FATHER'S
GEISHA

JAMES
GORDON
BENNETT

WASHINGTON SQUARE PRESS
PUBLISHED BY POCKET BOOKS

New York   London   Toronto   Sydney   Tokyo   Singapore

To my father
To the memory of my mother
And to my sisters, Gail and Eileen

Portions of this novel first appeared, in different form, in the following periodicals: "Dependents" in *The Virginia Quarterly Review* and in *New Stories from the South: The Best of 1987;* "The Sorrell Sisters" in *The Yale Review* (under the title "The Searle Sisters"); "In the Grass" in *The Antioch Review;* "Good Hearts" in *St. Andrews Review;* and "Pacific Theater" in *The Virginia Quarterly Review* and in *New Stories from the South: The Best of 1989.*

A Washington Square Press Publication of
POCKET BOOKS, a division of Simon & Schuster Inc.
1230 Avenue of the Americas, New York, NY 10020

Copyright © 1990 by James Gordon Bennett
Cover illustration by Pamela Patrick

ISBN: 0-671-74000-8

First Washington Square Press trade paperback printing December 1991

10 9 8 7 6 5 4 3 2 1

WASHINGTON SQUARE PRESS and colophon are registered trademarks of Simon & Schuster Inc.

Printed in the U.S.A.

I would like to thank Amanda Urban for the call and Lisa Bankoff, my agent, for staying on the line. It's been my great good luck to have Jane Rosenman as my editor.

CHAPTERS

The Army is a wonderful atmosphere in which to bring up children.

—NANCY SHEA,
The Army Wife

Fifteen minutes ago they had been a family.

—F. SCOTT FITZGERALD,
Tender Is the Night

DEPENDENTS

"Get real," Cora says when I ask her how long she thinks Daddy will stay in the BOQ. "Just lighten up, will you?" and she folds the page over on her movie magazine.

One of my father's MPs is substitute bus driver today. Waves of heat are already rippling above the macadam so he keeps the door open, which Cora says is against military regulations. Then as soon as we're past the guard hut, he switches on his portable radio. "Another Article Fifteen for you," my sister whispers.

It's a half hour from the Proving Ground to Yuma Grammar. Right across the river is California, where the times change ("You can say that again," Cora likes to say), but on the long ride into the city there's nothing much to see except the desert and the Mexican border. And so mostly the enlisted kids do their homework. Except Jeffrey Orr, who Cora claims is narcoleptic. The time he fell into the aisle and knocked himself unconscious, our regular driver, Corporal Greenspun, had to race back to the dispensary, and we were an hour late for school. Now everyone tries to get Jeffrey to take an aisle seat.

The only other officers' kids are the Sorrell sisters, who no one sits next to. Cora says it's because Colonel Sorrell is CO. Still, I believe that Leslie and Claudine are in love with me, even though we never sit next to each other on the bus.

When we pass the giant saguaro with all the bullet holes in it, I ask Cora what a "philander" is.

1

"Philanderer, knucklehead. Give me a break, for Chrissake."

Cora will be salutatorian of her eighth-grade class ("Only because Sheila Haggar gets credit for crap like Home Ec") and is an expert on all celebrity crossword puzzles. "Your sister is precocious," my mother will say to me. "She is also given to moods. *Nota benhay.*" When I tell Cora this, she makes her favorite snorting sound through her nose. "What mother means is *nota bene.*"

My sister is preparing for our newspaper's annual Oscar Awards Night Contest. Last year she tied for runner-up ("Big deal, a crummy *Yuma Gazette* T-shirt"). This year she will win ("Because I'm *sick* of finishing second"). The grand prize is again a week for two at the luxurious Riviera Hotel in downtown Las Vegas, air fare included, only one entry per family permitted. Cora jots notes to herself in the margins of her magazines. Whenever an Oscar nominee is mentioned, she underlines it in red ink. "It's all political," she'll say, uncapping her pen. "You have to know who's in and who's out. Or whether the vote's going to get split. Or whether they want to give it to a musical two years in a row. In other words, too complicated to explain to you."

My sister doesn't care to play ridiculous children's games, and so when I see my first road runner of the morning, I don't bother to shout "Beep-beep" before anyone else on the bus. Even though Beth Sibula and I are tied in points.

My mother says that things will work out and that I am not to take the cares of the world on my young shoulders. Cora says that I should hang loose or I'm going to have a peptic ulcer before I can shave. "Besides," she'll say, "it's not the first time Daddy's been in the doghouse." But this time is different. This time my father is a philanderer.

The public school where I am in the sixth grade is not, according to Cora, academically sound. The best teachers come from the post and leave when their husbands are transferred. Many of my classmates are mestizos who live in adobes and go to school barefoot even in the winter. They have black, shiny hair and brown teeth, and always smile when they try to speak English. They are friendly and seem happy but will never, my sister says, graduate.

When I get to homeroom, Miss Clark is wearing her red Chinese dress. The one with the slit up the side and the same one my father saw her in at PTA. Afterward he joked with my mother that he regretted more than ever having gone to parochial school. My sister nodded at me and said that I could relax. Daddy wouldn't be missing any more parent-teacher meetings.

Cora says that my homeroom teacher is a tease and that she's been egging on some hick rancher for months. Whenever I see her in the cafeteria, she is always eating alone. Miss Clark thinks I will make an excellent college student someday. In the meantime she wants me to try to get outside and mix with the other boys and girls a little more. But during recess I prefer to sit on the swings and talk to her, because like me, she chooses to keep to herself.

This afternoon, when I point this out to her, she tilts the swing back and smiles. Her hands are raised overhead to grip the chains, and her bare knees locked to brace her feet in the sand. Under her arms a thin crescent darkens her Oriental dress. She squints in the bright sunlight, making her seem when she talks to me to be concentrating fiercely. And I can pretend to be her rancher. Cora, who misses nothing, is the first to suspect this ("Just watch she doesn't string you along like her lonesome cowboy").

"Well, young man," Miss Clark says finally, bending her knees to allow the swing to carry her forward, "then we must both come out of our shells."

When she says "young man," my chest prickles the same way it does whenever the bus hits a road runner.

Saturday, my father arrives to pick up my mother. Somebody big is coming through, and there will be a color guard reception at the officers' club. As provost marshal, my father is required to wear his dress uniform even when the guest is a civilian.

"Must be hot stuff," Cora says, tapping the ribbons over his pocket. "Pop's all dolled up."

I no longer ask my father how he earned his decorations. He would only tell me once again what some pedicab driver in Korea charged him for his Silver Star. And if he hadn't run out of them five minutes before, it could have been the Medal of Honor. When I was a boy, my mother frowned upon his joking with me this way. I would repeat the tales at school and they would come back to her through the parents of my classmates. That my father's master parachute wings were won at the Mount Tom carnival in Chicopee, for example. Or that the scars on his knees only *look* like shrapnel wounds. He had, in fact, accidentally knelt on a red ant hill while on a picnic with "your mother."

My father hasn't been by in three days, and the hothouse tomatoes he set out on the windowsill are now ripe.

"Look at that baby," he says, palming the biggest one admiringly. "Cora, *le sel.*"

My sister hands him the shaker, wagging her head. "You get that on you, mister, your ass is grass."

But my father expertly slices the large tomato in half and jabs the saltshaker at it repeatedly. "I get one seed on me," he says, thrusting his square chin forward, "I take it out on your hide."

The juice only dribbles a little down his chin and he slurps it up with his tongue.

"Our role model," Cora says to me.

Although my sister tries not to show it, she is excited to have my father back. She spent the morning adding to the movie-star collage on her ceiling and tells him that it's ready for inspection. But before he can get up from the table, my mother is standing in the kitchen door.

"Hello, Major."

I barely recognize her voice. It seems deeper, almost hoarse. And it is the first time I've ever heard her call my father by his rank.

"Come for your tomato?"

Even Cora laughs at this.

My father scrapes his chair back. "I guess we'd better march," he says, clearing his throat. He seems as startled by my mother's presence as I am. Something more than her voice has changed.

"You can check out the room when you come back," my sister says, and hands him his braided service cap. "Assuming you *do* come back."

When my father glances sheepishly at my mother, she only rolls her eyes. "Your daughter, Provost."

As soon as the car backs out onto Truscott Circle, Cora is pounding me on the shoulder.

"Could you believe that getup? Un-be-*liev*-able!" She smacks her forehead with her palm. "Where did I see it? Give me a second." She closes her eyes dramatically. "It's coming. *Un momento.* I see it. I got it." She grabs my wrist and drags me into the living room. "Sit." And she pushes me onto the couch. "Remain seated."

I watch her race back down the hall.

"Mom looks as good as a spit shine," my sister calls out to me from her room. "That Kraut won't know what hit her."

Cora claims that the other woman is some German hausfrau, the wife of one of my father's young lieutenants. ("Dad's a xenophile— one attracted to foreigners, nine across. What can you do?")

My sister wanders back, flipping through one of her magazines. "If it's not in here," she says without looking up, "then it's . . ." But she's found it. "There," and she thrusts the picture triumphantly before me. "Who's *that* remind you of?"

I study the black-and-white photograph of a woman standing beside a large canopied bed. She's wearing only a slip and has one arm over her head, gripping the wooden post.

"Jesus," Cora says, snapping the magazine out of my hands. "It's Liz. Doesn't *Butterfield 8* even ring a bell?"

But all we get at the post theater are John Wayne and Wile E. Coyote cartoons.

"Mom's vamping him," Cora says, more to herself than to me. "Obvious to everyone, of course, except a certain idiot sibling."

But the contest entry form has to be postmarked by midnight, and she retreats to her room with her red ink pen.

In the carport I unzip my father's golf bag and scoop out a handful of balls. He keeps two sand wedges, and I take the older, scratched one.

There's an abandoned parade field just up the block, and I wear my nylon baseball cap. It's probably close to a hundred degrees out. They test experimental equipment at the Proving Ground. Like the cap my father brought home. Somebody from Quartermaster said it was the original prototype and that it cost a couple million dollars to develop. When I told my father that my Little League cap was more comfortable, he said I was what made America strong and that I didn't have to worry about ever being drafted.

Even on the parade field you have to keep your eyes open. My father's first sergeant once killed a sidewinder in his three-year-old's sandbox, and every other dog you see has a limp. "Why don't they test something nuclear?" Cora likes to say. "Meanwhile we could all go up to Vegas for a couple weeks, government expense. Come back when all the snakes are dead. I wouldn't have to win any stupid contest."

I try to keep my elbow stiff on the backswing. There's enough room to hit a driver, but it's too hot to do much walking. Every other week my father lets me tag along with his foursome. I'll hold the flag or replace divots. He didn't mention anything about this weekend, though. So I guess it's off. When he goes fishing, he'll bring me along, and I'll be the only kid. Even though some of his buddies have sons my own age. Still, I didn't ask him about Sunday. He doesn't have to think about me all the time.

The ball makes a little puff of dust where it lands and you can't take your eyes off the spot or you'll lose it. But when I see Leslie walking across the parade field toward me, I forget about the ball. Her younger brother trails behind her, tossing a play parachute into the air. She suddenly stops and points at the ground.

"Got it," she calls out to me.

I wave the club and pick up the other ball. I don't want to risk sculling it. While they wait for me, her little brother wraps the handkerchief tightly about the rock and hurls it toward the road. It doesn't open.

Leslie stands with her hands on her hips like a runner. She's taller than me but still has a flat chest. We both watch her brother stretch his arm out behind him like a javelin thrower. He makes a grunting sound, heaving the rock with all his might. The handkerchief comes down again without opening.

"I guess everybody's over at the reception," Leslie says, taking the club from me.

I don't ask her where Claudine is. If her sister isn't at home reading a book, then she's at the library looking for a new one.

Leslie nods at the ground and I drop one of the balls at her feet. In the distance her brother stops to watch her take several practice swings. She bends both elbows the way girls do but I don't say anything.

"Your mom and dad go together?" she asks finally.

Cora says that it's always going to be news when "the goddamn provost marshal's living in the BOQ."

"Yes."

She swats at the ball but it only skitters off to the right.

"You probably think track's pretty stupid for a girl, don't you?"

I watch her squat down and scoop some sand into a small mound. The fine blond hair on her arm shines like gold.

"Well," she says, "I can't help it if I'm good at it."

Looking up at me, she holds her hand out and I set the second ball in her palm.

"I should tell you what my mother said about your father." She balances the ball on top of the mound. "It's rich."

Her brother yells something to her, but she ignores him.

"She said your father's the only man around here who knows how to wear a pith helmet."

This time she hits the ball solidly, and it sails high over her brother's head.

After dinner Cora and I talk my mother into letting us see *The Comancheros* at the post theater. Even though the Proving Ground is several hundred miles square, you can walk to everything in ten minutes.

"Mom's a wreck," my sister says as soon as we leave the house. "That stupid Kraut was at the reception."

It's already dark enough out to see a few stars. And in another hour or so you'll be able to hear the coyotes. They like to wander down from the hills for any scraps they can dig out of the mess hall cans.

"Dad introduced them," Cora is saying. "So now they're supposed to go over for drinks. Mom's ready to shoot him."

I find the Big Dipper. "The lieutenant?"

My sister glances past me at the canal across the road. It's stagnant and thick with algae, and her lip appears to curl up at its smell. "Daddy, moron."

There is a long line at the theater, and Cora spots a baby-sitter we used to have up near the ticket window.

"Every man for himself," she says, and is gone.

Ten minutes later Sergeant Shuman sticks his head out of the double glass doors to the theater.

"Sorry, folks. All sold out."

They'll have a second, special showing at eleven if we want to buy our tickets now.

I don't much feel like a movie anyway so I'm not real disappointed. There's a *National Geographic* special on at eight about the Arctic. Or I could just read.

I take the long way home, past the Sorrells' house. Leslie reminded me that as dependents we could use the driving range at night. For fifty cents split a large bucket of practice balls. Because she is athletic, she'd probably learn to keep her elbows stiff.

All the streetlights flicker on ahead of me like new bright stars. It's dark enough to see satellites.

But then suddenly I am sitting in the road, the pavement still hot from the heat of the day. To stand I have to grip the stop sign before me. And as I pull myself up I understand that it's what I walked into.

At home my mother puts me to bed, wrapping several crushed ice cubes in a facecloth.

"Miss Clark says you're preoccupied," she says, pressing the facecloth to my burning forehead. "That you daydream in class."

We both listen to the coyotes howling outside. Usually, for something like this, my mother will say, "Like father like son." But tonight she doesn't.

Some time later I am awakened briefly by the sound of voices in the kitchen. The hushed tone makes me cock my ear. And then it is Cora, I think, who I hear. Or perhaps my mother. In the dark it's hard sometimes to tell them apart.

I was dreaming of the Arctic and of playing golf with Leslie in the snow. It was as flat and bare as the Proving Ground, and each ball we hit hung in the air like a miniature moon. "Don't even bother to look," Leslie had said, dressed in her track shorts and sneakers. "You're not going to find anything."

I slide up against the headboard, shielding my eyes from the overhead light.

"Honey, you want to get up?"

It's my mother. And then Cora is standing in the doorway, both of them still dressed.

"Too bad you're not on the ballot," my sister says to me. "This is Oscar-winning stuff."

My mother stares at the sheet covering my legs. "That's enough, young lady." But then just as abruptly her voice is gentle and coaxing. "Put your clothes on, sweetheart. I need you for something."

As soon as she leaves, Cora crosses her arms as if to mimic my mother's stance.

"Don't let an MP near her," she says. "Her breath could kill a steer."

My mother waits for me in the car, the engine already idling.

"You feel all right?" she asks, reaching over to touch the Band-Aid on my forehead. There is quite a welt. But the stop sign probably kept me from wandering into the canal and drowning.

Cora comes out of the carport to shout, "Headlights," but my mother ignores her, shoving the gear shift into reverse. I know where we are going. My father took the staff car. Now my mother will retrieve him from the duplex over on Stillwell Avenue. Cora pointed out the flat-roofed house to me from the school bus. "Mata Hari's place," she said, and then fogged the window to trace a skull and bones. Even though Cora is older, my mother brings me instead because I am the male.

"You don't want the wrong impression here," she begins, gazing

straight ahead. It is the kind of blank look she gets ironing my
father's khaki uniforms. "Your sister can get a little carried away.
Right now she's upset with your father. And she's probably said
some things to you."

I crack my window. Not even the cooler air at night keeps the
canals from smelling like rancid perfume. You can hear the frogs
croaking as if even they can't stand the stench.

"He just wants his men to like him," my mother is saying. "Only,
sometimes the social drinking gets out of hand." She glances over at
me as if to be certain that I've not fallen back asleep. "We both know
when to let Cora go in one ear and out the other."

My mother's voice grows sullen as we move out of the senior-
grade housing and into the low, flat duplexes of the junior officers.
I recognize the tone. It is the same one Cora uses whenever she
believes things have gone beyond her brother's feeble limits.

"You may have your father's coloring," my mother says as if I just
contradicted her, "but you've damn well got my eyes."

She concentrates on the straight road ahead but occasionally jerks
the steering wheel sharply to keep from crossing the center line.

"I know what you're thinking," she says without looking over at
me. "But I'm not."

The year before, her license was suspended when she accidentally
drove the Buick into the canal. It was late, and she'd taken the turn
off MacArthur Boulevard in third instead of second. The judge
advocate told her she was lucky she hadn't drowned, and then put
her on probation for six months. "Mom got off light," Cora told me
afterward, "mostly because Dad has the goods on guess-whose
sixteen-year-old?" The judge's daughter had been caught laminating
fake IDs for the PX.

My father's familiar green staff car is parked in the double
driveway of the duplex, and on seeing it my mother pulls up too
close to the curb, squealing the tires. She leaves the engine on,
looking first into the rearview mirror to wet down her eyebrows, and
then at me.

"Your head must be pounding," she says, and hooks her warm

hand around my neck to draw me toward her. "I won't be a minute, sweetie. Then we can all go home."

There is rum on her breath. Cora fixed her piña coladas in the blender.

"I hate him," I say, but my voice catches, garbling my words.

"What?" My mother grabs my wrist when I try to open the door. "Sweetheart, you just sit and listen to the radio. I won't be a minute." And then, as if she'd finally been able to decipher what I said, smooths the damp hair back from my forehead. "Your father's the bravest soldier in the army, honey. This doesn't mean anything next to that."

Cora likes to say that my mother is your basic just-taking-orders kind of housewife. But even my sister knows better than to break The Rule. We are never to bad-mouth our father in her presence. Never.

I slump down in the front seat and watch my mother, one shoulder lower than the other, walk up the yellow patch of lawn as if trying to get to the front of a moving bus. Her toes point, like my sister's, slightly out. Cora says that the lieutenant's wife is built like a tank and that Daddy is bored with being provost marshal and wants to get back into Artillery.

When at last the screen door is pushed open several inches, my mother steps back out of the way as if to accept the invitation to come in. Instead, she waits until my father joins her on the porch, wearing civilian clothes and holding a glass in his hand. I turn off the radio but their voices are too low to hear. In a minute my father disappears back inside the house, and the lieutenant and his wife replace him, framed in the light of the door. The lieutenant's wife is nearly as tall as her husband. And I think of Miss Clark standing in line at the cafeteria, the heads of her students barely to her shoulders. They are both smiling, talking to my mother as if still trying to win her inside. But she doesn't uncross her arms until my father reappears, this time wearing his leather aviator jacket even though it is too hot for it.

At the driveway he turns to wave good-night to the couple, who have come out onto the porch holding hands. My mother does not turn or wave or say another word to my father. She walks instead ahead of him past the staff car and around the lieutenant's MG.

As soon as she is back in the driver's seat, my mother pats me twice on the knee and tells me never to marry a WAC. Then she tries to turn the key in the ignition but the engine is already on. When the gears grind, she snaps her hand back as if from a snake.

"I know what you're thinking," she says to me.

My father ambles up alongside the car, stooping so that his chin rests on my open window. "Hey, buddy," and he taps his forehead with one finger. "You been back-talking the old lady?"

My mother looks coolly at him. "Step away if you don't want any toes flattened."

My father's tanned face shines in the dark. He grins happily, his straight, even teeth those of a movie star.

"Sure you don't want to come in?" he says to my mother. "They're right nice people."

"Don't patronize me," she answers sharply. "That's your son sitting there."

My father reaches in to grip my shoulder. "Then maybe I ought to invite him in. What do you say, soldier? You want to show your mother how to be sociable?"

He squeezes my arm as if to gain my attention but I haven't taken my eyes off him. I've never seen my father smile that way before. My heart is racing even faster than with Leslie.

"Don't you ask him that," my mother says. "Don't you ask him anything."

Over my father's shoulder I can see the lieutenant and his wife still waiting on the porch. They shift their weight from one foot to the other in the cool night air. But they can't close the door on us.

"No," my father says resignedly, and takes a single duck step back from the car. "We don't want a momma's boy."

Before I can even turn to see her, my mother has flung her door open and is shouting over the hood.

"What did you say, mister? What the hell did you say?"

I twist in the seat as she flashes by the rear window. But by the time I unlock my own door, my father is grasping both her arms, dancing away from her furious kicks.

"You bastard!" she is screaming. "You lousy bastard!"

The lieutenant trots down the driveway but stops respectfully at the mailbox.

"Sir?"

His wife stays on the porch, one hand at her mouth.

"Sir?" he repeats, but then looks away helplessly.

My ears still ring from the stop sign and I cover them with my hands. As if in pantomime my mother attempts to wrench free until my father trips over the embedded sprinkler head and they both drop to their knees in the scorched grass.

"Don't you come home," my mother says, her face only inches from my father's. "You don't live there anymore, mister."

"Fine," he says, wishing only to calm her. "Fine. Let's just call it a night."

But he doesn't follow her across the lawn.

When she staggers around the car, my mother glares at me menacingly.

"And the kids are mine," she shouts, closing her eyes as if to steady herself. "Mine."

Back again in the front seat, she rests her forehead on the steering wheel.

"I could drive," I say, even though at home I've never gone farther than the curb.

She lifts her head tiredly. "I'll get us there, sweetheart."

And she does, but not without first backing into the lieutenant's mailbox, crushing the little red metal flag.

At the house my mother pours herself the rest of the piña colada mix from the blender and goes to bed, locking the door after her. It is what she does whenever my father is left to sleep alone on the couch.

Cora tiptoes down the hall to peek into my room.

"Any stabbings?"

I pretend to be asleep.

"Army life," my sister says, easing the door shut behind her. She kneels on the throw rug beside my bed. "The civilian population doesn't know the half of it."

Over her head I can just make out the different model airplanes suspended by fishing wire from the ceiling. Several of the real ones my father has jumped from on maneuvers. Once, when I asked him how it felt to fall all that way before his chute opened, he said he'd be able to explain it better when I was a little older and maybe had a sweetheart like Miss Clark.

"Don't take it too hard," Cora advises me, one elbow on the mattress. "They'll kiss and make up. Mom's not going to let him rot in the BOQ." When my sister stands up, she tries to touch the damp pillowcase without me noticing. "Listen, you're just an army brat. You don't know the whole story yet."

At the door she whispers that if she wins the contest, she'll think about taking me along. "Who knows, Vegas might be good for you. Give you a shot at the big picture."

However, Cora doesn't win the Second Annual Oscar Awards Night Competition. An unemployed typesetter who once worked at the newspaper does. "Mostly they was just guesses," he tells the reporter from the *Yuma Gazette*. "I never even seen the pictures." My sister's letter to the editor, in which she demands an entire revamping of the contest rules, still hasn't been published.

The following week, right after I watch Leslie sprain her ankle in the hundred-yard dash, Miss Clark breaks her engagement and leaves before the school year is even over. She was fired by the principal, Cora claims, because he found her in the teachers' lounge smoking a joint. "Except, what really did it," my sister says, "was finding her in front of the floor fan in her half slip."

The day my father moves back in, Cora strings a banner outside the house that says, ALL HAIL THE CHIEF! then we pile in the car and go out for steaks. There's a popular restaurant in town where the maître d' cuts off your tie and hangs it from the ceiling with the thousand others already pinned up. In the parking lot my father puts on the paisley tie we gave him for Christmas. Only, my mother doesn't find it particularly funny.

Now that he's back, my father has started taking a lot of inspection tours. Weekenders to places like El Centro and the Gunnery Range across the border. At night you can hear my mother arguing bitterly with him. But this morning Cora sits beside me on the bus without having been told to. And for the first time she seems to consider things I ask her seriously. For instance, when I wonder what makes army families any different from the rest, she peels her thumbnail back so far, the skin bleeds. "Dad tries to pull off any more one-night stands," my sister says, scanning the desert as if for a road runner, "Mom'll show him what a civilian family looks like for a change. *Nota bene.*"

BRATS

To get out of serving on the Welcoming Committee, my father volunteers to go up with the Ranger class himself. Because of this my mother refuses to join the other officers' wives in the viewing stands, and only Cora and I sit in the broiling bleachers. But school is out and neither my sister nor I have anything better to do.

Down below, a bright red carpet stretches from the podium to where the guest of honor stands beside Colonel Sorrell, the post commander. When I wonder aloud who the guest might be, my sister looks up from her movie magazine (she carries them in her bike satchel), her tongue poking into her cheek.

"Probably some South American dictator. I can smell the after-shave lotion all the way up here."

A convoy of staff cars from El Centro and Luke Air Force Range are parked behind the bleachers, and I count the number with red flags attached to their bumpers.

"I can't wait for the day Dad gets his star," I make the mistake of confessing to my sister. "We'll have our own driver."

Cora is wearing her Lolita sunglasses but I can still see the contemptuous look in her eyes as she peers back at me. "And go where?" she says. "The Gunnery Range?"

The Special Services Band sits just outside the shade that shields the row of VIPs. Their starched khakis are black with sweat as we wait for the transports to come rumbling in from the airstrip.

17

Although my father joked about going up with a bunch of skinhead Rangers, he seemed pleased that Cora and I would be in the stands.

Only the South American dictator appears unfazed by the humidity. Through his interpreter he flirts with the young wife of one of the generals' aides.

"Look at that oily little bastard," Cora says, rolling her magazine into a baton. "He runs a country? He looks more like a Cuban dance instructor."

Lately, my sister's thyroid has been acting up and it's hard to tell whether it's that or just nerves that make her so jumpy.

"Okay," she says irritably. "Here's the sixty-four-thousand-dollar question." And she stops to gaze at the empty horizon for some sign of the first plane. But there are only clouds, great big billowing ones rolling in low from the east. The kind that will surprise you in the desert in late July. "What's Dad get out of all this?" she asked. "Fifty measly more bucks a month. I mean, did he ever stop to think why they call it hazard-duty pay? I'll tell you why. Because it's hazardous to your health is why."

This is what happens when my sister sits in the sun too long. She starts worrying like my mother.

"Dad's a soldier," I say. "It's his job."

But she isn't in the mood to debate. Not, at least, at the risk of heat prostration.

The band, meanwhile, plays another Sousa march, their arms wilting beneath the weight of their instruments.

The clouds have darkened by the time the loudspeakers crackle with static and an amplified voice directs our attention toward the jump tower. It's a moment, however, before the transports, too far off yet even to hear, loom out of the low-hanging rain clouds.

"They ought to call it off," Cora says anxiously. "Look at that sky. What if it starts lightning? They'll be fried before they hit the ground."

I count six planes and know that my father, being the ranking officer, will probably be in the lead one. On the wall in my room is a black-and-white photograph of him dangling his legs out of the open cargo door of a C-47. What makes it scary is that the plane is

ten thousand feet off the ground and he isn't wearing a chute. Cora
hates the picture. "You want to hero-worship," she'll say, "tack up
Steve McQueen. Steve jumps out of Rolls-Royces. He gets his
stand-in to do the moron stuff."

As the planes circle, I wonder what my mother is doing. Probably
the wash. The machine will drown out the jet engines. If she isn't
stuffing my father's uniforms into the dryer, she'll be sitting in front
of the television with the volume turned up. Just after Christmas my
father was supposed to join some of his junior officers for a fishing
trip to the Gulf. But when the weekend forecast called for a
small-crafts warning, my mother drew the line. If he went, he
wasn't to expect either her or the kids to be there when he got back.
After spending half the night listening to her slam dresser drawers,
my father finally gave in. The next day two of the men (my father's
adjutant and a second lieutenant) drowned when the rented cabin
cruiser sank less than a mile from shore. It's something my mother
never lets Cora forget whenever my sister accuses her of being overly
protective. But my father still claims it was because they were the
only ones who weren't Airborne Rangers.

"This is crazy," Cora says. Traces of heat lightning have begun to
flicker in the distance and she's persuaded that the airdrop should be
canceled.

Everyone in the stands is hunched forward, hands cupped at their
forehead, eager not to miss the first budding of chutes.

"What the hell," Cora says. "As long as we impress the crap out
of Cesar Romero."

At this the major's wife just below us twists about to tap Cora on
her outstretched foot. "You're a little young for that kind of
language, don't you think?"

Even before my sister lifts her sunglasses, I know what's coming.
Cora doesn't like to be touched. Ever. By anyone.

"I was speaking to my son," she says, looking down at the woman
as if at a piece of gum stuck to the bleachers.

Caught off guard, the major's wife tilts her head back, raising
both hands to shade her eyes against the sky's intense light. Even if
my sister isn't a child bride, there is always the chance she could be

a general's brat. But then, like a great clap of thunder, the band starts up again just as the C-47's rip through the clouds, bodies tumbling out of their cargo doors like bowling pins. And the woman turns her back to us, the roots of her bleached hair glistening with sweat.

I know that Cora only wants to distract herself from the sky's filling up with parachutes. The lightning worries her but she refuses to admit any chickenness on her part. It isn't the kind of ammunition to hand over to her next of kin.

"Thank you, Jesus," she says when the bandleader at last sits down. My sister still can't relax, her hands tucked beneath her thighs as the chutes stream from the backs of the planes.

Like tuning forks the men dangle at the ends of invisible cords.

It isn't something I ever want to do myself. I don't take after my father.

Without sunglasses I'm squinting narrowly when someone down near the front in the bleachers, a woman, I think, starts causing a real commotion. I'm trying to figure out what it's all about when Cora suddenly jumps up beside me as if for a foul ball. And then everyone is standing, arms raised as if at a revival and even the guest of honor is waving his swagger stick at the clouds. But I'm seeing double from looking into the sun and have to turn away.

As the first few jumpers hit the parade ground, they roll over to absorb the stiff shock of the hardpan. Puffs of dust rise from their heels as the silk chutes collapse about them like deflated hot-air balloons.

A second chorus of shouting wells up in the bleachers. Rows that resisted rising are all on their feet now, and I cup one hand at my brow, trying to train my eyes in the direction the others insist we look.

Beside me Cora makes a whimpering sound. Nothing more than a muffled "Oh," her fist at her mouth, as if she's about to be sick.

Then, an instant before it's too late, I catch the two chutes out of the corner of my eye: twisted into a single braid, twin figures no bigger than a thumb spinning about each other, spiraling at the end of the same ghostly knot, heads bent, arms up, legs pointed.

Already people are fleeing from the bleachers, while only a few hold on to hope, screaming their instructions. Their reserves, they should pull their reserves, they shout. But then abruptly it's over: the dull thump, a soundless crumpling. Like puppets they buckle at the waist, the entangled shrouds descending about them.

Cora has turned away and I sit down beside her now.

In the distance a small brown truck with a red cross on it already bumps slowly across the parade ground, dust curling up behind it. There is no reason to hurry. The chutes hadn't opened enough to make a difference, and I watch the last few Rangers sway gracefully in the sky, their own chutes perfect white cones above them.

Cora hasn't taken her hand from her mouth. Like everyone else she follows the slow progress of the truck until it disappears into its own cloud of dust.

The bleachers creak and are quickly empty. Down through the stands the ground is littered with mimeographed handouts. The airdrop was to have been only the beginning of the program. There was the precision flying team to follow.

"I guess they'll call off the rest of it," I offer.

Cora is clutching her sunglasses in her lap. There's a red mark on the bridge of her nose. And then she begins nodding her head as if admitting something to herself.

"It could be Daddy."

I am staring at her. She has the perfect profile of my father. The same fair skin. The same dark, thick hair. I look back down at my hands. They've begun to shake and I pin them beneath my legs. It's why we came. We're army brats. Yet we'd never seen our father, a master parachutist, jump before.

"No," I say, and my sister is suddenly shaking her head in agreement.

"There were hundreds," she declares. It's her Big Sister voice. "There were dozens in each plane."

"Daddy would know what to do," I say. "The others were only learning. One of them made a mistake."

Cora can't hide her pained expression. I must look pathetic to her. "Dad's made a million jumps," she says. "He packs his own chute."

The generals have moved off with their guest of honor. They stand beside the staff cars, shaking hands, looking solemn. Even the translator no longer smiles as he passes on the dictator's condolences.

"Let's go," Cora says.

We walk our bikes across the grass behind the bleachers. The area has been carefully policed. Everything scrubbed and edged. Even the large drum barrels given a fresh coat of paint, TRASH restenciled in white.

"There were at least three hundred," I say. "Fifty to a plane."

My sister continues out ahead of me. "Let's not ride yet," she says.

Heat lightning flashes beyond the jump tower as we bump our bikes over the concrete speed guards. Cars pass us slowly, some of them with their headlights on as if part of a funeral procession.

"What time is it?" Cora says.

Her voice shakes and she clears her throat.

"Two-thirty," I say, even though she is wearing her own watch.

We stay in single file. Heat waves ripple above the concrete like gas fumes.

"Let's find some air conditioning," Cora says over her shoulder.

She doesn't want to go home yet. Mom would know we were upset about something and start asking questions.

Behind us cars are pulling over to the side. It is the Red Cross truck come up the access road from the parade field. The driver eases over the curb onto the street without bothering with the siren.

We stop to watch it pass. I try to see in the small meshed window but it's too dark. Cora starts walking again and doesn't say anything until she comes up with the idea of catching the last half of the matinee. Dr. No is at the post theater. We've already seen it twice but my sister has made up her mind. After another block she straddles her bike and pedals off.

The breeze feels good and I think about my father. He is forty-one years old and already led a rifle company through Inchon and only come away with some shrapnel in his knee and neck. Which he just makes fun of, shaking his leg whenever it looks like rain. God wouldn't let some recruit's guidelines get mixed up with my dad's. If that happened then there can't be any God. But I'm afraid to say this to Cora. "Think about Jeff Chandler," she'd say. "Or Jayne Mansfield, for that matter." If accidents can happen to movie stars, what chance do the rest of us have? So I just ride behind her and keep my mouth shut, standing up on the pedals every once in a while to pump a few times before coasting.

In the dark, empty theater we sit on the aisle because Cora is claustrophobic. Sean Connery has already discovered Ursula Andress searching for conchs on the beach, and as soon as Cora sits down she starts mouthing the dialogue word for word. Half a dozen movie magazine subscriptions come to the house every month, which my father argues only fills my sister's head with fairy tales. But since Cora has always been at the top of her class, my mother wants to know who's doing any better than his daughter in school? Anyway, it's still a sore point between them.

By the time it comes to the scene where James Bond escapes from the island, Cora looks ready to go. Seeing her profile lit up by the screen, I'm reminded why people find it hard to believe that we are brother and sister. Even my mother has to admit it. "Your sister's your father's daughter, all right," she'll say to me. "But the two of you look like you came from different orphanages."

The lights go up in the theater before all of the credits have finished, which is one of Cora's pet peeves.

"Hicks," she says as I trail up the aisle after her. "Hayseeds," and she sails a flattened popcorn box at the projection booth.

Outside, Cora lingers in front of one of the posters for coming attractions, and I can tell that she wants me to leave her alone for a minute. So I walk down to the picture of Paul Newman leaning on a pool cue. After a while Cora comes up beside me and we both study the poster together without saying anything. But what I'm really doing is staring at my sister's reflection in the dull glass.

"If that was Daddy," she says without turning to look at me, "I'm coming back and burning this place down. I'll pour gasoline everywhere. And I won't care if some spec-2 janitor's still inside either." The tears curl down to her chin but she ignores them. "You can come with me if you want, it doesn't matter. I'm just telling you what I'm going to do."

My sister can scare me when she wants to. As she's scaring me now. But we're both afraid to go home.

Cora lifts her front tire out of the empty bike rack. She's wearing her Dick Clark Caravan T-shirt. Last month my mother drove us up to Blythe to see a rock and roll concert. She thought it would be a good way to get Cora out of the house and for us to do something together as a family (my father was on maneuvers). But my sister isn't interested in Dick Clark or *American Bandstand*. While all around us kids were screaming at Fabian, Cora only looked over at my mother and me and yawned. These weren't real stars, she wanted us to understand. These were rock and roll stars. You only saw real stars in the movies.

We're less than five minutes from the house and as I pedal beside my sister, I keep trying to think of something else we can do. The lanes are just thirty-five cents a string until six, but Cora hates to bowl. The only thing athletic she'll even consider is swimming, but, of course, we don't have our suits. And as we cross Truscott Circle, I think of turning back and hiding out in the post library but already we're picking up speed, coasting down Gavin Hill, my heart racing. Cora is standing up, her hair whipping about her head, and just by keeping her bike out ahead of mine, I understand that in her own way she means to look after me. Whatever we are riding toward, she'll be first to arrive at. She only needed a little extra time at the theater to prepare herself. My sister is braver than me because I'm not strong enough to nudge my front tire out ahead of hers. She will be the one to stride up to the front door of our duplex and if there is already an MP there or Dad's CO or a priest or even Mom crying, she'll turn and put her arm around me. I'm her younger brother and that will be her duty.

At the top of Eisenhower Street we can see the house for the first time. There is no provost marshal's car out front or anything official-looking from the motor pool. But then they could already have come and gone. Dad had been picked up by a driver. So it doesn't mean anything that there is no staff car around. We were at the theater over an hour.

At the curb we walk our bikes up the driveway and quietly lean them against the side of the carport. After a moment Cora thinks better of it and pries her kickstand down. She isn't ready yet and so I pretend to check the air in my tires. The backside of her shorts is pressed with the outline of her bicycle seat. She seems to cock her ear toward the dining-room window but there is nothing to hear. And as my sister steps past me, I want to reach out and hold her. But I don't, of course, because she doesn't like to be touched.

A staff car suddenly pulls up in front of the house, and Cora moves back beside me, looping her arm over my shoulder. My sister is half a foot taller than me and three years older but it is the first time I can remember her ever giving me anything like a hug. And I nearly lose my balance. Staff cars have green tinted windows, so we can't really see anything as it sits idling with whoever is inside in no hurry to get out.

When at last the passenger door swings open, my sister lowers her arm and steps in front of me so that I can't see the car. Afraid to look past her, afraid to see what she's already seen, I concentrate instead on the delicate cracks in the concrete driveway. Like a road map they zigzag in every direction. And I think of how many times we've followed the blue then red lines in the road atlas to our next assignment. Always at night with my father driving, my mother on the lookout for a motel with its neon vacancy sign still blinking. Cora bored and flipping through her magazines with a flashlight. And me massaging my father's stiff shoulders, watching his drooping eyelids in the rearview mirror. I know perhaps better than even my mother how his dark hair smoothly dovetails to hide the thin white scar of shrapnel.

"Oh," my sister says, and as I look up she turns, her expression as blank as if she's only holding the phone out for me. Then she steps back beside me and together we watch the man walk up the driveway toward us, his crisp khakis bloused at the boot. But my eyes have watered and he's wearing dark aviator sunglasses so it isn't until he smiles that I catch my breath.

"Some show," my father says.

My sister only stares up at him until her whole body begins to shake and she turns quickly to walk back to the house alone.

When the screen door slams shut behind her, my father lifts his service cap off and brushes one hand through his damp hair.

"I called your mother," he says as if to apologize. "No one was back yet."

I reach out to take his cap from him. His name and address are printed inside. But it is just like him, I think, not to include his rank.

"Your sister gets carried away," he says. "It's those damn movies."

I curl my fingers under the lining of the headband. The thin leather feels cool and moist. I'm thinking how flushed Cora's cheeks had been, as if she'd just run several blocks in the heat. Her eyes were shining. She hadn't wanted us to see her cry.

"Nobody's fault," my father says finally.

And I can't tell if he means Cora and me not knowing or just the chutes not opening.

"You see enough of these things," he says, still sounding apologetic, "you're going to run into this."

He takes his sunglasses off. The knuckles of his left hand are scraped and bruised, but it isn't anything that was there this morning.

"The funny part is," he says, and already I know that he only wants to smooth things over. He's frightened us badly and now he wants it all forgotten, "—I never even went up. They couldn't get the damn thing off the ground."

It's a lie, of course. But I don't want him to feel any worse about it. So I don't say anything and instead just start making wishes to myself the way I sometimes do. Mostly they're old ones like my father never going overseas again without the rest of us. They're not things you can say out loud. For instance, like wanting him always to love my mother and my sister and me as much as we love him. But even I know that my father can't make any of those promises.

At least not without crossing his fingers. Except, walking up the driveway with him, clutching his service cap with both hands, I don't care. He's my father and he's here and that's all that matters. "Army families are all alike," Cora will explain to me later, decorating the margin of her celebrity crossword with tiny penciled parachutes. "Which is why they have to keep us moving."

THE
SORRELL
SISTERS

My father's transfer has caught us all by surprise. We've been stationed at the Proving Ground for nearly four years, our longest assignment in one place. Now suddenly we're called upon to live apart again. After nearly two weeks of indecision my mother has decided that the rest of us will move to Los Angeles until my father's tour is over.

"All we ever get is the dregs," Cora complains. "Why couldn't it be England or Europe? Why does it always have to be some godforsaken outpost?"

This is ridiculous, of course. Just another popular misconception Americans have about the Far East. But when I try to argue that Taiwan is different, my sister looks up from the mound of shredded newspaper on the floor. "See what happens when they get a library card too soon?" Cora has been miserable our whole time in the desert and so L.A. is my mother's concession to her. I write my sister's prickliness off as just another effect of her condition. Whenever her thyroid flares up it's best to give her a wide berth.

Because my mother refuses to fly, my father is forced to take a week off from his hectic schedule to help with the drive. He wants my mother to know that this puts a tremendous professional strain on him and that he expects quid pro quo. Cora, the only one to have gone to a Catholic school (half a year in Ottawa), translates this as being basically a threat. Since we won't have a moment to lose, my father wants to be able to leave the office and step into the station wagon with all of us ready to hit the road.

"It's his whole attitude," my sister grumbles, wading through the excelsior in the living room. "Like we're a bunch of privates or something."

My mother wraps her favorite bone china in newspaper. "Your father's got a lot of pressure on him right now," she says. "It's no picnic for him either."

"Everybody's got this idea it's a rain forest," I say. "Actually, the capital gets—"

"Give me a goddamn break," my sister says.

My mother runs her damp sponge down the strip of masking tape. "I don't want to hear any more," she says. "I want the two of you back to work on your rooms. Now."

On the stairs my sister elbows me in the side. "Think about it," she said. "Your first French kiss could have been with a Chink."

"All right," my mother calls up to us. "I mean it."

In my room I take down the Raquel Welch poster. I hung it over my bed because it irritates my sister but also because it reminds me of the Sorrell sisters. Not that Leslie or Claudine looks like a cavewoman from one million years B.C. They just have the same kind of high cheekbones and long legs as the movie star.

But even though it's the Sorrell sisters I'll miss, it's my parents I worry about. My father's assignment has caused a lot of friction between them. Lately, every conversation seems to end in a stony silence. Cora is predicting a permanent separation ("I've seen the movie"). I've tried to be a comfort to my mother ever since the orders came down. And more than once she's told me how much she relies on my good sense. So I feel badly whenever Cora manages to goad me enough that my mother has to step in.

I stand by the window and look out at the cactus in the backyard. It's July and at night you can hear the coyotes, who know the pickup schedule of the Corps of Engineers. Saturday mornings there will be the usual litter of overturned garbage cans up the street.

I unplug the rock tumbler and take out all the stones. They shine like marbles, and I set them on the windowsill, where you can see their sheen in the sunlight. I'll miss the desert. Where else can you trip over an entire petrified tree on the way to school? You never know what to expect out here. "Except skin cancer," Cora will say. "That and second-run movies." But nothing seems to entertain my bored sister anymore. She gave up a long time ago even trying to make new friends.

I wait by the window. Leslie sometimes takes the path behind the house because it's a shortcut to the golf course, where she likes to jog. I can't keep up with her for more than five minutes before the first dagger cuts into my side and I have to put on the brakes. "Eat more bran," she'll say, running backward, her blond hair glinting in the sun. "Get more sex," I call back after her but not quite loud enough to be heard. "Wait till her knockers come in," my best friend Mick likes to say. "It'll improve your stamina." After being held back a year for poor academic performance, Leslie started an intimate diary, parts of which she permits me to read. My favorite entry is where she pierced her own ears in the girls' locker room after a track meet. But what I like best about her is the way she leans against the chain link fence after a softball game and says, "See you, Teddy," whenever my mother pulls up in the station wagon. And in the car I'll glance back to see her waving after me, one knee cocked, her foot pressed against the fence. "You're too young to worry about girls," my mother will say, adjusting the rearview mirror. "Keep your mind on your books. There'll be plenty of time for them later."

Now, I think, flopping down on my mattress, there won't be any more time for Leslie. Not to mention Claudine. Dark, quiet, studious Claudine. "That one at least has some semblance of a brain in her head," Cora will admit. Claudine belongs to Choral Society, but I was told that my voice ("How should I put it, dear?") hasn't quite formed just yet. Perhaps I should come back next year. But next year, as it turns out, I'll be a thousand miles away and not even on an army post. Despite her quick mind Claudine wasn't chosen for Debate. "Mr. Andrews doesn't think I'm aggressive enough," she told me after tryouts. "And he's probably right. I'm not like my sister. I don't run after what I want." Later, when I thought about it, I decided that Claudine had been flirting with me. She has a roundabout way of saying things, but I determined that in the future I'd try to be more attentive, not allow certain things she says to go over my head. Even if she *is* nearly three inches taller.

When I come back down from my room, my mother is putting all the photo albums in pillowcases.

"I thought we'd bring a few along in the car with us for conversation," she says.

"We haven't driven that far together in a while," I say. "I mean, what's it going to be like, the four of us on the road again?"

"Hell," Cora says. She's come out into the hall upstairs. "Sheer, unmitigated hell."

"Have you two made up?" my mother says.

"What's to make up?" my sister says. "It's his fault."

She's changed into shorts. Only, there is something else different about her. It isn't until she follows me into the kitchen that I realize what. Her eyes are rimmed with pencil liner.

"What're you staring at?" she says.

"What do you think? You look like a raccoon."

She stands in front of the cabinet, squinting at her reflection in the glass. "I barely touched them."

"With what? I say. "A tarbrush?"

She sits down at the Formica table.

"You're the only one in this family I can get an honest answer out of," she says. "Everybody thinks I'd wilt and die."

I know what she is going to ask. For the ten thousandth time my sister wants to know if her eyes bug out. It's the reason she spends most mornings in front of the bathroom mirror experimenting with mascara, eye shadow, and even fake lashes. My mother has warned me that my sister is sensitive to criticism right now and that I'm to try to be generous about her condition. But anyone can see that, in fact, her eyes *do* bug out. And not just a little. Her overactive thyroid is to blame and there's no hiding from it.

"They're no different from the last time you asked," I say finally. "And the last time you asked, they weren't any different from the time before that."

"Not froglike or anything?"

As a matter of fact that is exactly how they look. But I know better than to be the only one in the family to be honest. Sooner or later my sister will have to face the truth. Meanwhile, my mother argues, our job is to be gentle with her. That is what families are for.

I pour myself a glass of milk and try to picture the Sorrell sisters' eyes. Leslie's, I am fairly certain, are hazel, but Claudine's are a mystery. She rarely seems to look directly at me.

"I asked you a question," Cora says.

She wants to know if any of my friends, Mick, for instance, has ever said anything.

"About what?"

"Jesus," and she gazes up at the kitchen ceiling. "About my eyes, idiot."

"We've got better things to talk about."

I know that the more belligerent I am with her, the more convincing I'll likely sound.

She scrapes her chair back from the table. "Pretty impressive mustache. Too bad it's only milk."

I wipe my arm across my mouth, tempted to say something spiteful. But then it would be just like my sister to get me mad enough to tell her the truth.

I promised to meet Mick after lunch, and as soon as he sees me crossing the ballfield he sends a high fly towering in my direction. I raise my glove to shade my eyes but lose the ball in the sun. After a long, scary silence it thumps in the dirt at my feet.

"That was close," Mick says as I come down the third baseline. "I mean, another foot or so . . ."

I sit down in the dugout.

"You need to stay closer to the ground," Mick says finally. "It's what makes it so hard to pick up the ball when you're running." But it isn't really his nature to give advice, and he can see how shaky I am from almost getting clobbered. After a while he narrows his eyes at me, his broad shoulders arched back, his head slightly turned against the sun. He looks like his father, a staff sergeant who raised him like a recruit. "Heard something," he says, the bristles of his crew cut stiff as a hairbrush. "Something interesting."

I feel the dark pocket of my glove where my mother's sewing-machine oil has stained the leather. "What?"

Mick smiles at me. "Sheila was on the upstairs phone this morning. My sister has a big mouth."

I know the feeling.

"They're all sleeping out at the Sorrells'," he says. "They're using my dad's old service tent."

It is like another ball just missing me. "Leslie and Claudine's?"

Mick laughs. "Sheila spent twenty minutes on the phone trying to figure out how to get the poles over there. Like it was some kind of prison break or something."

I walk out to the mound. It feels good to be standing in the sun. It's a dry heat without any humidity. The desert sky is always blue and when it rains it's over quickly. The weather is the one thing you can count on.

I look at my friend standing at home plate, rotating his shoulders with the bat under his arms. He is the best player on our team. The only time I've ever seen him strike out, the pitch was at least six inches high but the ump refused to reverse his call. Even after both the third base coach and our manager stormed home, faces red and hats waving. Only Mick returned to the dugout without protesting. It isn't something his father ever wants to see from him. You don't question authority in the military, you don't question it on the ballfield.

"A slumber party," Mick says, tapping his cleats with the end of his bat. "Could be interesting."

There is no problem sneaking out Friday night. I've done it before. My father flew in from an inspection tour this morning and spent most of the day arguing with my mother. Cora went to bed early after taking her medicine. The dosage has been upped again and it makes her drowsy.

On the back porch I stare at the dark shapes of the saguaro that poke up like hatracks on the horizon. The black sky glitters with

constellations. I am still star-gazing when a pack of dogs skulk out
of the desert and cross the road. But they are too scraggy looking
and slump shouldered for dogs. And I know they are coyotes. Come
down out of the hills the night before garbage pickup. There are
warnings in the daily bulletin about rabies and so I keep upwind of
them. After a while, behind me, I hear the clatter of aluminum cans
in the street.

The tent is pitched in the open and brightly lit from within by a
lantern. The girls' silhouettes flutter against the canvas like shadow
puppets. I stand for a moment, trying to make out their voices. But
they all seem to be talking at once, at least half a dozen of them,
kneeling or sitting cross-legged on their sleeping bags. When,
suddenly, something the size of a dog moves up beside me and I
lurch backward.

"Just me," Mick whispers. And he smiles his familiar gap-
toothed smile. "Can you believe this? A tent full of girls."

It's something to see, all right. But my breath has already been
taken away, and I have to sit still a moment longer, hand over my
heart as if for the Pledge of Allegiance. Every once in a while the
cicadas shriek in waves like banshees. There is the stench of the
canals, the scum on top like lily pads. In only a couple more days,
none of this, I know, will be there for me anymore: not the stars, not
the desert, not the Sorrell sisters.

"You okay?"

It's Mick leaning over me. I hyperventilated.

"You skip dinner or something?"

Over his shoulder a cactus flickers like a compass needle.

"I don't want to move," I say.

Mick nods. "You hurt yourself?"

But I only meant from the Proving Ground.

"It's like some kind of henhouse," Mick says at last. "They haven't
shut up since I got here."

Colonel Sorrell must have been the one to put up the tent. The
canvas is as taut as a drum, with mosquito netting draped over front
and back. Every few minutes one of the girls lifts the lid on the ice
chest and opens another soda.

"You wonder when they come up for air," Mick says.

We can't really make out what anyone is saying. Just a lot of squealing and giggling. But as we crawl closer, their voices become more distinct. Besides Leslie and Claudine, I recognize Penny Allen, Nancy Fisher, Ann Innis (whose father is post chaplain), and Mick's sister, Sheila. You can tell they don't have any plans to go to sleep. They're excited and all talking at once.

Mick and I lie facing the street. If Colonel Sorrell decides to check up on his daughters, that is the direction he'll come. But I doubt he is too worried. There's practically a female squad in the tent.

After a while they settle down enough that you can follow a conversation. That is when I begin to feel a little guilty. It is like listening in on somebody's party line.

Mick lies on his back looking up at the stars. He doesn't seem at all troubled. Just bored. He's heard his sister before.

I only listen to hear Leslie's voice. Claudine rarely says a word. She is reading *Women in Love* and every so often stops to share a passage she thinks the others might like.

After nearly an hour Mick has gotten a kink in his neck and wants to go. But then Claudine suddenly flaps her book shut. "Sometimes I think Lawrence understood women better than we understand ourselves," she says.

"Isn't he the one who's so queer?" Penny says.

The others laugh, a harsh, collective laugh of derision. They are tired and the tent is cramped and they'd rather be at home in their own beds, comfortable and asleep. You can hear it in their groggy, slightly hoarse voices. They are still best friends, of course. Only things have gone on too long. That is in their voices too. They are getting on each other's nerves. Especially Claudine, who is smarter than the rest of them and just a little prissy about it with her nose in whatever boring book.

"Queer as a three-dollar bill," Nancy adds.

"Maybe a little like your boyfriend," Sheila says.

Now even Mick sits up.

"I don't know who you're talking about," Claudine says. She's opened her book back up as if to ignore them.

"Does the name 'Teddy' ring a bell?" Ann says.

I glance over at Mick. He's drawing circles in the sand with a stick. At the mention of my name the others laugh that same cruel laugh. And I think that my heart has stopped. I can hear everything. Can picture Claudine's quick, sharp intake of breath.

"You don't think your teddy bear's a little queer?" Penny says.

"His family's the one that's queer," Ann says.

"What's wrong with Teddy?" Leslie says. She's held back, caught between her friends and her sister.

"Maybe you're the one should tell us," Sheila says. "You two hang around so much together."

Claudine smooths the page out in her book. "Just ignore them," she says.

Leslie waits for the others to stop laughing.

"They're moving," she says finally. "So what's the difference?"

"You're not going to miss him?" Penny says.

"Why should I?" Leslie says. "We're not steady. Anyway, who cares?"

"You're going to be able to sleep without your teddy bear?" Sheila says.

"I'll live."

Then Ann says something I can't hear and in a moment they're all giddy again and hurling pillows at Leslie and tumbling about on their sleeping bags.

Penny at last sits up, catching her breath. "You ask me, I think his sister's the queer one."

"Cora?" Claudine says.

"She hardly ever leaves the house," Ann says. "Who ever sees her?"

No one says anything.

"That's what I mean," Ann says. "She doesn't have any friends. She's like a hermit."

"I guess I'd stay inside, too, if my eyes looked like that," Nancy says. "She's got some kind of disease."

"I'll tell you why they're leaving," Penny says. "His parents are getting a divorce."

"Mom said that a long time ago," Leslie admits.

"Tell us something new," Ann says. "Everybody knows that."

"Except maybe Teddy," Nancy says.

"Even my dumb brother feels sorry for him," Sheila says. "He says he's the worst player on their team. All he does is daydream out in right field."

Mick suddenly stands up, signaling for me to follow him. *It's only girls talking*, his pained expression seems to say.

"My sister's a jerk," he says as soon as we are out of earshot. He bends over to pick up a rock. And for a moment I'm afraid he's going to throw it back at the tent. But he only flicks it into the canal. "She doesn't know what she's talking about. None of them do."

We keep walking. "They were just shooting the breeze," I say.

But he doesn't look at me again until we get to the road. Then we both stop.

"I guess I'll see you tomorrow," Mick says, dusting his hands off.

I can't think of anything else to say.

"Well, anyway," I say finally, and shrug my shoulders. "Thanks for coming."

In the distance the water tower stands like a giant golf ball on top of a tee. There are off-limits signs but the chain link fence has never kept anyone out. The tower's crazy alphabet of graffiti even includes my own spray-painted initials. But I don't know any Jane who's supposed to love me.

I'm sweating when I drop to the other side of the fence. My heels hit the concrete hard and I feel the same cool tingling up my spine as when Ann first said my name. The metal ladder is at least seven feet off the ground but with a running start, I catch the bottom rung and start up, rust coming off on my palms. There's no wind but I don't look down again until I duck under the railing and am sitting on the wide catwalk.

It's a clear night and I can see Cassiopeia directly over the girls' tent. They still haven't turned off the lantern. The canvas glows like a small white triangle in the desert. My own house I can barely make out. A black square just beneath Andromeda.

I got what I deserved for sneaking. Lately, it's become a habit. It's all I seem to do around my parents. So I had it coming. But how else am I supposed to find anything out? For once I know how my sister feels. No one, including her brother, ever tells her the truth. All she has to do is look in the mirror. She really *does* look like that. Her eyes bug out and her throat is as swollen as an inner tube. She isn't pretty anymore and never will be again. That's the truth but none of us will tell her.

I can stand up and gaze down through the iron mesh of the catwalk. It's what I get for snooping, all right. But so what if my father doesn't love my mother? So what if he doesn't love any of us? What is he supposed to do? Tell the world? Why should he have to be the first to tell anyone anything in our family? No one else ever does. I close my eyes and lean over the railing. Maybe things will be different with him in another country. Maybe he'll get homesick with us in L.A. I bend my knees and teeter-totter on the metal bar, knowing that if I tip forward too much or even just open my eyes for a moment, I'll tumble over, and so I keep them closed, which seems the only way to keep my balance.

VOICES
I
LOVED

Cora squints at the oncoming headlights, brushing the tears from her cheeks roughly. She isn't used to crying in front of me.

"If you really think you can keep this from them," she says bitterly, "then it wasn't your tongue that needed stitching."

I'm still numb from the Novocain and too tired to write anything down. One of the nurses found a small chalkboard for me in the all-night gift shop.

"No week in a national park's going to turn them into newly-weds," my sister says, accelerating up the entrance ramp. "They'll be back at each other's throat before they pull into the driveway."

There is only one reason she hasn't already called the lodge. And that's because just yesterday I came in on her smoking pot in her bedroom.

But she starts nodding at the rearview mirror as if to convince herself that she hasn't been compromised in any way.

"If I want to tell Mom you bit off half your tongue, I'll tell her. Got it? They left me in charge, mister. Which makes you the minor and me the major."

However, I know that whenever my sister is bluffing she talks faster, and she's been going nonstop since we left the emergency room.

"I mean, what am I supposed to say when she tells me to hand you the phone?"

41

I keep the blackboard in my lap. She isn't really asking my advice.

"And just guess who's going to get strung up alive for this?" She flashes her brights at the van in front of us. "Move over, moron." The driver drifts out of the passing lane and Cora darts past him. "I'll be grounded so long, I'll forget how to drive."

My sister is hyper, and not just from worrying about what she's going to tell our parents. She's still shook up from the accident. I was out late sitting in the tree house when the plyboard suddenly opened beneath me and I seemed to fall forever, arms jackknifed overhead, until something seared my chin, snapping my mouth shut thickly.

I woke up with Cora aiming a flashlight at me in the ligustrum.

"Oh, Jesus," I heard her say. She couldn't keep the beam from jumping. "Oh, Jesus, Teddy."

My Disneyland T-shirt looked like a butcher's apron, splinters sticking from my chin like a goatee. But it was the little red leech stuck to my forehead that dropped the flashlight at my sister's feet. She rushed back into the house to empty a tray of ice cubes into the blender. When I opened my eyes again she was packing the severed tip of my tongue in a sandwich bag of crushed ice. It glowed like a goldfish in the moonlight. I could hear the station wagon idling in the driveway but after testing my weight, Cora decided instead to back the car right up to the side of the house. She hadn't called for help, either an ambulance or the neighbors. We aren't a family to ask favors.

It's after midnight when we get back from the hospital, and my sister has only her mute brother to talk to. Sitting down on the edge of my mattress, she picks up the postcard from my bed table. It's a picture of a car driving through the hollowed-out trunk of an enormous redwood. Beneath Mom's *Miss you* my father has printed the names of the three largest sequoias: Generals Sherman, Grant, and Lee.

"I guess they'll stop off in Tahoe," Cora says. "Must be nice without the brats."

My father has been in Taiwan over a year now and this is his first hardship leave: three weeks with the family.

Later, Cora comes back in and sets a TV tray down before me. It's an unaccustomed role: serving her invalid brother. She's heated up some of the soup Mom put in the freezer for us.

But I've lost any sense of taste, and the coordination of swallowing has become tricky. There's no feeling until the soup is halfway down my throat.

"That character they brought in to do the stitching," Cora says, and yawns deeply enough that her eyes glisten. "An absolute ringer for John Carradine. Not to mention looking half-tanked the whole time."

I study my feet at the end of the bed. They're sticking up under the sheet like a headstone.

My sister kicks off her leather sandals, her white socks grass-stained from when she ran out into the yard. "I mean, it's not like you'd be an orphan or anything. They'd still be your parents, for God's sake."

I take up the chalk and rub my pajama sleeve across the clouded blackboard. But my tears begin to roll down my cheeks.

"You need anything," Cora says, backing out of the room, "just whistle."

The next night my mother calls collect from the Lodgepole Visitors' Center.

"Practically in the clouds up here," she says after I carefully raise the other phone in the upstairs hall. "Your father's in seventh heaven. How's your brother doing?"

"Who cares?" Cora says with remarkable casualness. "He doesn't listen to a word I say anyway. Now he's got laryngitis to prove it."

"What're you talking about?" my mother says, and already I can tell that she regrets the trip. "It's the middle of July. Put him on."

"That's the thing," my sister says. "He can't really talk. His voice is shot. It'll probably be a couple days."

"He's lost his voice?"

"He never listens. I told him to stay out of that idiot tree at night. So, that's what he gets."

"Your weather's been good," my mother says. "I check it in the papers. What're you telling me? It's been sunny all week. Lows in the seventies."

"It has," my sister says, and I can't help admiring how confidently she lies. "He went out after his shower with his hair wet. Anyway, it's his own dumb fault. At least I'll have a little peace and quiet for a change. There's that."

"Put Teddy on," my mother says sternly.

When Cora tries to object, my mother stops her. "Get your brother on this phone. Now."

I wait for my sister to call me before pretending to pick up the extension.

"He's on," Cora says from the kitchen.

"Hello, sweetheart?" my mother says. "You really can't manage to say anything?"

I have to cover the receiver while I fight back a torrent of tears. My mother's voice has reminded me of the hopelessness of ever believing that she and my father will return to us any happier than they left.

"Probably not real smart to strain it," Cora offers.

My mother seems to consider this for a moment. "I don't like it," she says finally. "I don't like it one bit. And if I find out there's some kind of shenanigans going on . . . Just suffice it to say you'll wish there hadn't been."

She's going to hand the phone to my father now but first she wants Cora to know that she's calling Mrs. Grosset from across the street as soon as they hang up. And if she gets any kind of a different report, then she's calling back. "Pronto."

"Teddy, honey," she says sweetly, "you listen to your sister now and I'll call again when we can talk."

Then she passes the receiver to my father, mumbling something to him in an unfriendly voice.

"How you guys doing?" He sounds cheerful and rested. But then, my father rarely sounds any other way. "I take it we're a little under the weather."

Cora is still smarting from her conversation with my mother and only grumbles in response. Undeterred, my father happily goes on to describe one of the terrific trinkets they're working on over in Taiwan: walkie-talkies with TV capabilities. Platoon leaders or even tank commanders will be able to view each other in the field.

But I want to ask him how it's going with Mom. Whether the trip is helping them see things a little more eye to eye. But, of course, I can't.

"Well, listen," he says at last. "This is costing your vacationing parents, so let me hand this back to your mother."

I haven't been able to tell what kind of mood either of them is in. My father's hearty phone voice never seems to change, and my mother is too upset.

"There's nothing else you want to tell me, then?" my mother says to Cora.

My sister trusts only one defense. "What's the dif?" she says curtly. "You're not going to believe a word I say in the first place."

But there are all sorts of things I want to say. Only, ours isn't the kind of family you say them in. It wouldn't have made any difference if my entire tongue were missing. I know that nothing that really matters ever gets said between us anyway.

Five minutes after my mother hangs up, Mr. Grosset is on our doorstep. His wife has sent him over in her stead.

"*Bonanza?*" Cora says.

He nods. Mr. Grosset never seems to leave the house without a tie and jacket on, even though he's been retired for years. "She can't stand to miss a minute of that ridiculous thing."

Cora shakes her head. "You know why Ben Cartwright's sons have three different mothers? Because the old man's been widowed three times. If I were the next Mrs. Cartwright, I'd get the sheriff to look into that real quick."

I know that my sister won't have any problem with our elderly neighbor. Lately they've become fast friends. All because, two weeks ago, Mrs. Grosset mentioned to my mother that she and her husband once knew the same person everyone is reading about in the papers these days: Dr. Carl Coppolino.

"So, you keeping up with the trial?" Cora says.

It's the same question she asks each time she catches him hobbling down his driveway for the paper.

"I guess it's who I'd want for my lawyer," he says.

F. Lee Bailey is defending the doctor, who's accused of murdering his lover's husband. But the part my sister likes best is that the victim was a retired army colonel. The medical examiner performed an autopsy after the body was in Arlington for three years. Now the headlines are saying that the colonel was strangled.

"I guess it's true what they say about old soldiers," Cora says. "Apparently they don't fade away either."

Mr. Grosset smooths his white hair back with both hands. "It's all very suspicious, isn't it?"

Cora turns her palm up. "Anyway, I give you my dumb, in every sense of the word, brother."

I stay on the couch and Mr. Grosset gazes nearsightedly in my direction. The table lamp is off and Cora has dabbed some of her makeup on my chin.

"Well, he looks all of a piece to me," he says. "Your mother will be happy to hear it."

"From someone other than her impeachable daughter," Cora says.

Mr. Grosset pats her on the shoulder, something I know that my sister dislikes.

"Sylvia and I should travel," Mr. Grosset says to make conversation. "Only, to be truthful, I've never been a big fan of such things as water spewing up from the ground."

"Makes two of us," Cora says. "Give me Vegas any day."

"But I suppose when they're four of you involved, you're in for certain compromises."

"Right," my sister says. "Like leaving two of them behind."

Mr. Grosset makes his way over to me and I stand up. All I have to do, Cora has coached me, is keep my chin down and my mouth shut.

"Losing something like your voice," he says, "it puts things in perspective." And he squeezes the back of my neck like a doting uncle. "That's what happens when you get to be my age. You start losing all your senses, but everything's in perspective."

Although he means to be funny, everything he says always has a certain edge to it for me. My mother told us how their only child, a boy, died of some exotic disease when he was an infant. Dr. Coppolino had been the anesthesiologist.

"I'll pass the word on to your mother," Mr. Grosset says finally. "No adult supervision required."

"It's a test," Cora says, smiling at him even though I know that it's meant for me. "They want to see how we handle a broken home."

I push my tongue against the back of my front teeth. The tip still feels more like an earlobe: dull and slightly detached. And I wish that my sister's cruel teasing felt the same way. That somehow the Novocain could have deadened my feelings as well. But everything she says about us as a family seems as sharp and stinging as the needle had going into my tongue.

The next day, just to get out of the house, Cora drives us over to the diner near the Varsity Cinema. I've been up most of the night with a fever, flipping around in bed trying to fall asleep. Twice, Cora came in and held a damp facecloth to my forehead. She never said anything but I could tell that she was worried. The intern who looked like the movie star had told us that everything depended on how the muscles healed. "Whether he has a slur," Cora said, her own voice trailing off. The doctor then pointed his penlight into my mouth. "An impediment, yes, possibly," he said, turning my jaw to admire his handiwork. "Too soon to say." Sitting on the examining table, I held the magnifying mirror up to my face for the first time. The ugly black stitches zigzagged across my tongue like the tracks of my miniature railroad. When I opened my eyes again two nurses were peering down at me. "You passed out," one of them said as an orderly swept shards of glass into a dustpan. "My brother's prone to hyperventilate," I heard my sister say from somewhere else in the room. "You don't want to hand him any more mirrors."

There are only half a dozen wobbly stools in the diner and we sit at the end of the horseshoe counter. The only other customer is asking the waitress if she remembers all the tips he's left her this month.

"Didn't they do *The Killers* here?" Cora says, tucking the menu back behind the napkin dispenser.

I look at her blankly.

"*Film noir?*" She rolls her eyes. "Forget it. What're you having?"

I point to the small pen-and-ink drawing of a milkshake.

"Right," she says. "Something liquid."

The waitress comes down to us and swipes the counter with a dishtowel. "How you folks doing tonight?" She makes a face at Cora as if to say she gets characters like that all the time.

After taking our order the waitress rips the page from her pad and sticks it to the ventilator hood above the grill. The cook folds his newspaper in half and glances up at it without ever turning his back from us. Meanwhile, the man who's been heckling the waitress bites into his hot dog, lifting his chin to keep the sauerkraut from dripping. He alternates from watching the waitress's legs to gazing over at us without much interest. The grill hisses like a steam iron each time the cook presses the spatula down on Cora's hamburger. I tuck my knees in and spin one complete rotation on the stool. When I put my elbows back up on the counter, the man is staring at me.

"What's the matter, buddy?" and he wipes his chin with his sleeve. "Cat got your tongue?"

He takes another large bite out of his hot dog and works his jaw vigorously without closing his mouth.

Cora finishes cleaning her fork off with her napkin and smiles at me. "So show the man what the cat did to your tongue," she says, dipping her spoon into her water glass.

The waitress stops filling the saltshakers she's lined up on the counter and looks over at us. Even the cook turns and I see the rest of the faded blue arrow tattooed to his forearm.

After thinking about it for a minute I rotate a quarter turn and watch the man lower his hot dog as I slowly slip the tip of my tongue between my pursed lips. His eyes cross slightly as he leans forward on the aluminum stool, his own lips parting until he blinks and snaps his head back.

"Christ!" And he glares at Cora. "What the hell!"

My sister wraps the paper napkin about her spoon. "Cat got his tongue."

The man pushes his plate away from him and looks about as if to find the manager. But there's only the cook jiggling the cage of fries in the hot grease.

Afterward, we cross the street to study the coming-attractions poster outside the theater.

It's an old Art Deco place that only shows classic movies. Tonight it's something called *Daisy Kenyon* with Joan Crawford. The poster shows her in a low-cut dress with a neck pendant. "I don't belong to any man" is emblazoned across the top in red letters. The dress reminds me of the one my mother packed for the trip, the one Cora joked about being so practical for the road. But my mother didn't plan to spend much of her time sweating in the woods. So she'd folded the cocktail dress on top of a pair of slacks and white cotton socks. "Be prepared's Mom's motto," Cora had said. My mother only winked at me. "Remember that," she said.

Neither one of us wants to go back to the house.

"It's dollar night," my sister says to me. "What else have you got to lose?"

There are only two other couples in the deserted theater, but I have trouble paying any attention to the black-and-white movie. It isn't until Cora gets up to visit the ladies' room that I realize my leg has fallen asleep. My sister comes back with a box of popcorn and a Hershey bar for me.

"Thought it was something you could manage," she says without taking her eyes off the screen. "My God, look at those shoulders." Cora unfolds the top of the popcorn box. "You got to admire that in a woman."

When Dana Andrews gets into his car and drives off angrily, I can't help thinking about my parents. They were driving hundreds of miles away to see if they could come back together. But Cora had warned me not to get my hopes up. "Those two can't see the forest for the trees. Hitting the road's not going to get them anywhere except a damn park." Still, I wanted to believe that a change of heart was at least possible. That in perhaps forgetting about us they might think about themselves for a change.

As we come out of the theater the diner is lit up brightly across the street. There's no one at the counter, and the cook is scraping the spatula across the empty grill.

It's after eleven and Cora is worried that Mom might have tried to call.

"Maybe I ought to give them a quick ring," she says. "In case they've been trying the house."

It's started to drizzle, a fine mist that you can only see looking up at the streetlights.

"I can't wait not to have to answer to anyone," Cora says, hunting through her pocketbook for the number.

There's a pay phone on the corner and she turns her collar up. "Why don't you take a hike," she says. "You don't want to listen to Mom bugging me about her teddy bear."

In another six months, maybe a year, I'll be as tall as my sister. But rising only slightly on my toes I can already look her in the eye. Even if I don't have anything to look her in the eye about.

I wait beneath the awning of a jewelry store and stare at the diamond rings behind the protective metal gates. The more expensive ones have been taken in, leaving gaps in the velvet trays.

On the ride home Cora is quiet and I imagine at first that she is only thinking about the movie's unhappy ending. When she rolls her window down, her hair whips about her head crazily, and I keep my lips pursed, afraid that the breeze might catch my tongue the wrong way. Earlier, I made the mistake of sucking on some salted popcorn.

"Probably I ought to say something before you get carried away," Cora says finally.

I look over at my sister, who glances up at the rearview mirror as if I were sitting in the backseat.

"Apparently it's raining there too," she says. "Cats and dogs."

She is stretching the words out, which makes me think that for once she isn't bluffing. But I hate the familiar, Big Sister tone.

"They're coming back early," she says. "Tomorrow, as a matter of fact. They're both miserable. Mom's legs are supposedly killing her. Anyway, it's just not working out."

Her hair keeps flying into her mouth, and I stop listening when she starts in on why it's better that they go their separate ways. That with joint custody we'd get twice the benefits and only half the grief.

I turn on the radio. My sister is famous for being theatrical, for making a big production out of nothing. Next, she'll probably do her Katharine Hepburn routine and tell me she's going to have her tubes tied and never own anything that she has to feed or paint. I've heard it all before.

But back home she instead switches on all the patio lights and only stares out the kitchen window at the tree house. It's a shambles. The whole floor caved in under me.

"Getting a little old for stunts like that, don't you think?" When she turns around, her eyes are shining. Then she presses the back of her arm against her mouth and takes a deep breath, her whole body shaking. "So he goes and tears half his goddamn . . ." She leans back against the sink, her face contorted and angry. "Jesus, Teddy!" And she bows her head as if everything is hopeless: Mom, Dad, her brother.

I consider putting my arm around my sister's shoulder but, of course, don't. Instead, I open the cabinet drawer and pretend to look for something, pushing the utensils about noisily. I know that I'm not fooling anyone but then we aren't supposed to cry in front of each other either. And for once I wonder where all our family's unspoken rules come from. There seems to be one for every occasion and yet what good has any of them ever done us? But then it isn't the kind of question to ask and so I pick up the chalk and quickly scribble *Good night* across the board.

Upstairs, I hold the magnifying mirror under the desk lamp and try to curl my tongue. Even if things work out, there will still be a deep scar, one to hide whenever I smile. I'd climbed into the tree house to think about what it would be like not to live under the same roof with my parents anymore. Instead, I thought of the first time we were on our way across country to a new assignment. This was ten years ago and everyone was happy. My father because he'd just been promoted. My mother because my father was happy. My sister because she'd be starting a new school. And me because we'd stopped the car for a picnic. It was a small public park with shaded tables and a sparkling stream that ran through a thick stand of pines. Still too early for lunch we had the place to ourselves as I flapped around in the ice cold water in my underwear. It was so clean and clear that I could see minnows flash past at my feet like tiny tongues. But what I remember most was kneeling on the smooth stones with the water tickling my neck and suddenly looking up to see my mother and father and older sister together on the redwood bench, smiling happily, but without ever taking their eyes off me for a second. And so when the bough beneath the tree house broke and my arms shot out like a baby's, my hands clutching at whatever might break my fall in the dark, it was just as I'd felt on the phone, closing my eyes, listening to voices I loved, now too far away ever to hear me the same again.

OUT
of the
PICTURE

"I got some bad news for you, kiddo." Cora stands on the ottoman, using the same tack holes from last time to pin the sheet up. We're still in L.A. Still in the same stucco bungalow we've been renting and none of the furniture is ours. "Not even Hollywood families are forever."

I plug the projector into the extension cord. I know that my sister is just mad that we're not going to Panama. My father has been transferred to the Canal Zone, and my mother still won't budge. She's afraid the assignment won't be permanent and doesn't want us changing schools every fifteen minutes.

My father has sent another box of slides with his letter. The old ones I keep wrapped in tinfoil in my dresser so the sunlight won't fade them.

"You going to get her up or what?" Cora says.

My mother sleeps during the day and stays awake most of the night. She worries about all the crime stories in the supermarket tabloids, the ones Cora buys for the horoscope. But I don't know which stars my sister believes in more: the ones in the sky or the ones over in Bel Air.

"Come on, get Mom."

She wants to see the house my father has found. In his letter he talked about maybe hiring a cook and a maid. This was for my mother's benefit. For my sister's benefit he joked about how

Americans live like movie stars with the exchange rate the way it is. He didn't have to say anything for my benefit.

At the end of the hall I ease my mother's bedroom door open. "Mom?"

Even though it's the middle of July she sleeps under a mound of blankets.

"Everything's set up for the slides," I whisper.

From habit she keeps to one side of the double bed. "What time is it, honey?"

"Almost six."

She sleeps in her bathrobe, which Cora argues is the first sign of a depressive. But I just think she misses my father.

"Did you get something to eat?" she asks.

"I fixed us a salad."

Cora claims my mother is a dead ringer for Tammy Grimes, whoever that is. The streak of silver in her hair looks like something she had done at the beauty parlor. "I got that when you were a baby," she'll say to me. "You fell out of the high chair and broke your collarbone." Other times it will be Cora's fault. "Your sister was five. I'd just punished her for something. And when I wasn't looking she took my sewing scissors and trimmed the living room drapes. Cut them two feet off the floor all the way across." That sounded like my sister, all right.

My mother pushes the covers back and curls her toes. "My legs are numb. They must not be getting any circulation."

Like Cora, my mother is sloppy and I have to pick up after both of them. There are empty glasses and saltine wrappers everywhere.

"I'm going to tell you now," she says, draping over her shoulders the cotton shawl my father sent from Portobelo. "I don't want a repeat of last time. I don't want you getting yourself worked up all over again. Do you hear me?"

I hear her.

"I'll pull the plug on that machine the minute I see it. I'm not kidding. And I'll tell your father no more slides."

In the kitchen I fix cheese and crackers and carry the tray into the living room.

"Any chance we get to see these this calendar year?" Cora says. She flings her movie magazine across the coffee table.

The square of light is too low on the sheet and I slide the magazine under the front leg of the projector. My mother and sister stare expectantly straight ahead, their faces pale as Kabuki dancers' in the reflected light.

Drawing the loader back, I feed the projector the first slide.

"Focus," Cora says.

My mother reaches past her for the cheese. "Just hold your horses. Your brother's doing fine."

I cup the lens and turn it until my father's favorite subject comes in more sharply. It's a sunny day and the great concrete locks are bleached white. "How's that?"

"Boring," my sister says. "Boring, boring, boring."

It's the Gatun Locks. You can see the lake, the second biggest artificial lake in the world.

"How many times do we have to tell him?" Cora says. "No more goddamn canal."

"Watch the language, young lady," my mother says.

"You talk about home movies," my sister says bitterly.

"You might as well settle back and relax," my mother says. "It won't be the last one."

And it isn't. Most of the slides are of ships inching through the locks. Or of water rushing out of one of the giant gates.

My mother isn't much interested in any of this, either, but sits patiently for the one or two slides that will include my father. He'll have to hand his camera over to someone else, of course. Which he hates to do.

When at last my father appears in a slide, he is deeply suntanned. There are a couple of Americans with him, standing slightly back, clearly happy to be in his company. And for a moment I am so proud of him that I have to look away. But I know better than to change the slide too soon. There would be an instant howl of protest from Cora. So with my mother and sister I gaze at my father's face that is bigger than life on the wrinkled sheet.

"Can you believe that tan?" Cora says finally. "He must be living outdoors."

My mother's voice is barely loud enough to hear over the hum of the projector. "He'll get too much," she says. "He doesn't know how to do anything in moderation."

One of the younger men beside him, I suddenly notice, is holding a beer bottle.

"It must be some kind of outing," Cora decides. "An office party or something."

There are two women in the picture, both in the background. They look Panamanian.

"Your father's always been one of the boys," my mother says. "It's just the way he is."

"What's wrong with that?" I say.

My mother turns on the couch. "Nothing, sweetheart." She's squinting into the light, surprised by my tone. "I wasn't criticizing your father."

"Where are they?" Cora says. "I don't recognize any of this."

There is another slide of the canal before a second one of my father kneeling on a large straw mat, an ice chest at his feet.

"What's that?" Cora says. She gets up for a closer inspection and the slide ripples across her back like a tattoo. "Some kind of dock?"

When she touches the sheet the picture sways and we wait for it to settle.

"Those are rods," I say. "By the tree there. You can see the reels."

"Leave it to your father to find a fishing hole," my mother says.

"I wish just once he'd give us a few clues," Cora says. "He never says a word about anything. Like we're supposed to be cryptographers or something."

"What's there to tell?" I say. "You can see what they're doing."

My sister glares at me.

"Okay, honey," my mother says, and I set another slide in.

But it's only the locks again without my father.

"I didn't know they had country like that," my mother says. She's still thinking about the last slide. "It just shows you how you can get the wrong picture."

The branch library nearest us has a whole shelf on the Panama Canal. One Saturday I read how there were still headhunters in parts of the Darien jungle. But I didn't say anything to my mother. She wouldn't have been able to sleep even in the middle of the afternoon.

"Let's go," Cora says.

My father stands in front of a plain clapboard house, the fronds of a banana tree drooping over its red tile roof. It's a small house. The carport doesn't even look big enough for an American car.

"You're telling me there's going to be a live-in maid?" Cora says. "Where's she going to live-in?"

The grass in the front yard is yellow, and my father is holding his hand up to block the sun.

"Let's see what else we've got," my mother says at last. She glances over her shoulder to check how many slides are left. It's against the rules to preview any of them before the projector gets set up.

"Two more," I say, and pull the loader back.

Cora groans at the picture of the traffic circle in downtown Panama City. Hundreds of colorful taxis swirl around a statue of some Indian holding a tomahawk and a peace pipe.

"Let's go, let's go," my sister says irritably.

My father isn't in the last slide but at least it's another one of the house. This time taken from the street.

"I don't see any window units," my mother says. "You think there's air conditioning?"

"He's got a damn flash," Cora says. "I mean, what the hell's the place look like inside?"

"They probably have overhead fans," my mother says without taking her eyes off the slide. "But I can't handle the humidity the way your father can."

My sister gets up to turn on the light. "He thinks he's being funny," she says. "I've come to that conclusion. All that jackass *National Geographic* crap."

"All right," my mother says.

"It's like he has no conception of us whatsoever," Cora says. "Two pictures of the house and the rest of that idiot canal."

"What do you care?" I say. "You don't even want to go."

"So what if I don't?" my sister says. "That doesn't mean I wouldn't come home on vacation. If there were something to come home to."

"You ought to know your father by now," my mother says. "He'd sleep in a tent if I didn't watch him."

"Well, it looks like a neat house," I say. "It looks real private." I say this because I know how much my mother likes her privacy.

"You're right, honey. Your father didn't mention anything about neighbors, did he?"

"So what's new?" Cora says. "Daddy never mentions anything about anything to us."

But my sister is only angry because no one will say whether she can board in the States next year. If we stay here my mother will want her to commute. If we join my father, then she'll have to do her senior year in the Canal Zone. Only, no one seems to know what we're doing as a family.

"Who's fixing something to drink?" my mother says, lifting her feet onto the ottoman. "My gams are killing me."

I'm in the kitchen emptying ice cubes into the blender when Cora pushes open the swinging door and waits for it to settle shut behind her.

"So what do you think?" she whispers.

My sister is suspicious about something but I don't even try to guess.

"About what?"

She studies the picture of the four of us that's stuck to the icebox with little fruit magnets. "About Mom and Dad, blockhead. You think she'll just call it all off now?"

"Call what off?"

My sister rolls her eyes. "What do I have to do, paint a picture? What'd you think all the boys were doing down by the river? Fishing?"

Last May my father flew up for a week's leave. The day before we saw him off at the airport, my parents had another fight. Because it was late, they closed their bedroom door after them. But you could still hear my mother shouting about junkets and the children and finally about lawyers and custody. "It's only Mom letting off a little steam," my sister said when I got up from our long session at the Ouija board. "Relax. You're not going to be an orphan." And, in fact, the next morning my mother seemed to have forgotten all about it, even though her face looked puffy and swollen.

"Who do you think took the picture?" Cora says. "The Tooth Fairy?"

Sometimes I don't even know what wavelength my sister is on. My father believes that Hollywood's to blame and that she lost it at the movies.

The Coke cracks the cubes in the glass and fizzes noisily.

"Anybody could have taken it," I say, and then make the mistake of taking a sip of my mother's drink. It burns the tip of my tongue along the ragged scar. "Maybe he just used the self-timer."

My sister places the tiny banana magnet so that it looks like it's coming out of my ear in the picture. Then she seems to change her mind about what she's going to say and instead just nods. "The self-timer," she says, still bobbing her head at me. "Now, why didn't I think of that?"

When I carry my mother's drink in to her she's studying the framed picture of my father that's always been her favorite. It was taken the summer she was pregnant with Cora. "And your sister was a pain even then," she likes to joke with me. "Unlike her brother, who never gives me a minute of trouble."

My mother sits on the couch, and Cora and I watch her sip at her Coke like an invalid.

"So," she says. "What's to watch tonight?"

As usual, my sister has already gone over the listings in the *TV Guide*. "Nothing," she says. "*The Rains of Ranchipur* and some western with Nick Adams. They're not even worth turning on."

"Let's take a ride, then," my mother offers. "I feel like rubber-necking anyway."

Lately, it's all we seem to do together at night: drive through Beverly Hills or Brentwood with the windows rolled down while

Cora reminds us who lives where. She's taken the celebrity bus tour of homes a million times.

My mother walks back through the house, turning all the lights on. She leaves the TV and radio going and lifts the phone off the hook.

I sit in the backseat of the station wagon. Even though it isn't a new car, the army would still pay to have it sent down. If we went down. They would have paid to have it sent over to Taiwan too. Now all our stuff is in storage waiting for my mother to make up her mind. But she's afraid of Panama turning out to be just another short-term assignment.

As we cross Wilshire Boulevard into Westwood, Cora points out Jimmy Stewart's place. And my mother eases up on the gas pedal for us to take in the enormous, hacienda-like mansion with its terra-cotta roof and elegant palms.

"It's a wonderful life," my sister says dreamily.

This is when I miss my father most. The last time he was home on leave, Cora bugged him to drive us up into the Hills. Afterward, we stopped at a Baskin-Robbins off Rodeo Drive and while my sister recalled the size of some movie director's helicopter pad, my father dug into his chocolate-chip sundae. "Mmmmm, mmmm," he said, winking at me across the marble-top table and then licking his spoon appreciatively. "Not even Paul Newman's going to get ice cream any better than that. What do you say, Teddy?" I didn't, of course, have to say anything. He feels the same as I do about Cora's movie stars.

We don't go over to Coldwater Canyon tonight even though my sister wants to see how far Zsa Zsa Gabor has gotten rebuilding her house that burned down in the last brushfire. My mother's legs are bothering her too much. I carry a little tin of aspirin in my pocket for her and reach over the seat with one.

"You're a godsend," she says, her eyelids hooded the way they get whenever she isn't feeling well.

It's after ten by the time we pull into the driveway. But before anyone gets out, my mother flicks the brights on and revs the engine a couple of times to be certain there are no prowlers.

"Wouldn't one of Cora's horoscopes have warned us?" I say.

My sister doesn't even bother to turn around.

When my mother's at last satisfied that no one is waiting for us in the hedge, I lead the way up the flagstone steps to the porch. It's all ridiculous, of course, but my heart is still pounding as my mother quickly double-locks the door behind us.

In the living room Cora flops down on the couch. "If we lived someplace like Holmby Hills," she says, "we'd have our own private police department. Not to mention escort service."

"Maybe you'll marry a general when you grow up," I say. "Then you can take the celebrity tour of homes in his staff car."

"We'll see who gets the last laugh," my sister says.

The Ouija board has told her that she'll marry someone with a European accent. "Like the count in *The Sun Also Rises*." She means the movie, not the book. "Gregory Ratoff played him. You can have your Jake Barneses. They never have two sous to rub together."

Later, after we've gone back through all the old slides that include my father, my mother gets up without saying anything and wanders into the kitchen for a drink.

"You can't tell me she's that thirsty," Cora whispers, trimming her thumbnail with her teeth. "She's just anxious, that's all."

"And I guess her legs don't really hurt her either," I say.

My sister inspects her nail before looking back up at me. "Is this where I get to explain the obvious to you?"

Cora thinks that it's all just psychosomatic with my mother. That her physical ailments and her fear of flying are only symptoms. The real problem is with Daddy.

My mother suddenly backs out of the kitchen with a paper napkin wrapped around her glass. "I guess I'll lie down if there's nothing on TV," she says. "My tootsies are giving me a real hard time of it tonight." She raises her chin at me. "I want to talk to you a minute before you go to bed, honey."

I change into my pajamas first and when I pass Cora's room again she's sitting cross-legged on her bed, eyes closed and fingers resting lightly on the planchette.

"I don't know what I'm going to do with your sister," my mother says as soon as I close the door behind me. She's propped the pillows up against the headboard. "You can see how hyper she's getting."

Lately, whenever my sister's thyroid acts up, she refuses to take her pills. She complains that they swell her face up so that she looks like Orson Welles. It's only one of the reasons she keeps to herself so much.

"You can't talk to her," my mother says. "She won't even try to get out and make friends. It's not as if we're only going to be here for the weekend. She's had plenty of opportunity."

My mother is right, of course. Cora does nothing but sit around the house like she's serving a sentence. Her empty room even looks like a prison cell, the walls covered with pinups of movie stars.

My mother sets her newspaper down. "I know what's got you so quiet lately," she says. "You're worried your father and I are having a hard time of it right now. And we are. I'm not going to lie to you. But I want you to promise me something."

I know what she's going to say. "That I'll stop worrying."

"That's right," she says patiently. "That's all I'm going to ask you. Let your father and me handle it."

Cora is holding up slides to the light when I come back down the hall.

"Where'd you get those?" I say.

She hunts through the pile she's dumped out on the card table. "They're communal property. You don't own them." She gets up to turn off the overhead light. "Anyway, I wanted to show you something. So just start the projector and don't have a conniption."

"Start it yourself. I've seen them."

My sister straddles the extension cord. "You're missing an education," she says. But she doesn't know how to work the machine and jams the first slide so that only part of it appears on the sheet. "That's what you're getting," she says, jiggling the loader. "Half the picture."

I push her hand away. "You'll scratch them doing that." It's the slide of my father standing with some people outside a basilica.

"Good," Cora says. "Now, pay attention."

She's picked out three others.

"This one here," she says, the back of her head blotting out my father's face. "Try to remember her." She points at a young Panamanian woman standing on the steps of the run-down church. "Even if they all do look alike."

In the second picture my father is leaning on a rail in front of an animal cage. He mentioned the Colón Zoo in a postcard.

"So?" I say. There's no one else in the frame, only the striped tapir turned away from the camera.

"You don't notice anything?" Cora says. Her eyes shine in the light from the projector. This is what happens when she doesn't take her medication.

I pick up the last slide but she stops me.

"The bench, knucklehead." And she pats the sheet with the back of her hand. "What're you, blind?"

Beside the concrete walkway is an iron bench with a woman's jacket folded over it. When the picture stops waving, Cora narrows her eyes at me.

"Now go back to the first one."

I don't have to. It's the same jacket.

"Okay," my sister says. "Go ahead."

The last one is of the outing. Only, this time I concentrate on the dark-haired woman and not on my father.

My mother suddenly steps out into the hall. "I thought you were watching TV," she says.

Cora yawns. She's always been good at not looking caught. "We wanted another peek at the house."

My mother's a little nearsighted and I wonder how much, if anything, she can see.

"I'm going to bed," I say.

"Good," my mother says. "You'll get a headache looking at those things too much."

Later, it's after midnight and I haven't been able to fall asleep when Cora pokes her head into my room.

"And not a creature was stirring." She has two pieces of cheese and holds one out for me. "Want some?"

"Dad has all kinds of people working with him," I say. "But you have to make a big production out of everything."

"Been thinking about it, have we?"

Her eyes bulge from the pressure of her thyroid. She's supposed to take one pill in the morning and two at night.

"You can stay here, for all I care," I say. "There'll be that much more room for the rest of us."

"In that house you'll need it." She's close enough that I can smell the cheddar on her breath. "Anyway, kiddo, I thought I'd give you a little sneak preview. So the time comes, it's not a real shockeroo. But you don't want to see it, you don't want to see it."

I turn my head away from her on the pillow. "You want to do me a favor, shut the door."

Afterward, when I can't sleep, I start thinking about how different things would be in Panama. Living so close to Hollywood, you can't help seeing a movie star every once in a while. Last week, for instance, in Hamburger Hamlet I sat in a booth across from Lee Marvin. He wasn't eating anything. Just drinking coffee and reading the paper. I didn't tell Cora. I never tell her when I see someone. Not even the time I passed Debbie Reynolds in a crosswalk. If I say anything to my sister I'll never hear the end of it. But I was tempted to lean over the booth and ask Lee Marvin a few questions about his family. Whether, for example, he finds it hard on his kids for him to have to travel so much. Only, I wasn't sure if he even had a family, so I didn't ask. Anyway, he has a right to his privacy.

Sitting up in bed, I fumble in the dark for the alarm. But, in fact, it's the phone making all the noise. And then Cora is pounding on my door.

"Wake up," she shouts. "It's Daddy."

In the hall my mother and sister press against each other, their ears joined Siamese twin–like to the receiver. They smile blankly at me as if drugged by the voice at the other end of the line.

It's only the second time my father has called in over a month but already I can see that they've forgiven him. It's two in the morning and Cora is a little giddy. Only my mother is wide awake. It's the middle of the afternoon for her.

When at last it's my turn to take the phone, it seems forever before my father's voice carries the thousand miles to America. "Your mother tells me you're a big help to her," he says. "That's good news, son. You got to look after the girls."

My mother and sister loiter nearby, ears pricked to overhear the wonderful sound of my father's voice. But all I can think to ask him is about the time he went to the zoo and whether he had fun.

"Nothing like the time we're going to have," he says.

And then with Cora frowning at me I ask who he went with and whether that person had a good time too. It seems forever before he answers and not just because there's such a distance between us. It's even longer than that.

"Wait till you get a load of the frogs down here," my father says. "They're this bright yellow. Millions of them sitting on water lilies. Over in El Valle."

I think at first that we just have a bad connection. He isn't answering anything I ask him. Then finally he tells me to put Mom back on. And that I'm to take Cora with a grain of salt.

"You know how she gets," he says. "What do you say? Man to man."

But I don't have anything to say and only hand the phone back to my mother while my sister glares at me.

All the air-conditioning vents are closed in the hall, and I lean back against the bathroom door, trying to remember the dream I was having just before the phone rang. Research and Development had come up with a new kind of cable that was going to earn my father his first star. "It'll carry as much information as a forty-inch-thick copper wire," he explained to us happily. Then he reached over and plucked a strand of hair from my mother's head. "No thicker than this." We all stared at the silver strand stretched like wire between his fingers. Instead of electricity the cable would carry pulses of light. "And that's where the promotion comes in."

In the kitchen I stand in front of the sink and let the water run. Then I try to remember my father ever calling me "son" before. It had sounded like something in a foreign language.

After a while I hear my mother tell Cora to sit with her brother for a few minutes. When my sister wanders into the living room, I pretend to be reading one of her magazines.

"You're such an idiot," she says, curling her legs up under her on the rug. "See if I ever tell you anything again."

I look back down at the magazine but my eyes water and the tears start to pat on the page.

"Jesus," Cora says. "Do you believe *everything* I tell you? I mean, when I told you Charles Laughton was probably a woman, did you believe that too? Don't you know when I'm only thinking out loud?"

But I'm not really listening to her anymore. I'm trying to overhear my mother on the phone. Only, she isn't saying much. At least not enough for me to figure anything out.

Cora isn't fooling anyone either. All the time she's jabbering at me she keeps one ear open. My sister still believes she can get away with anything. But I've been onto her a lot longer than she thinks.

My mother at last joins us in the living room and tries to look cheery. Except I can tell that it isn't her legs that are troubling her.

"Who wants to take a spin around the block?" she says. "You two look more awake than I am." And she smiles anxiously at Cora, who stops whistling and slaps the *TV Guide* shut. My mother wants to get her out of the house. "What do you say? We can drive by that boarding school."

Cora sits up front in the car and pops her gum, her feet pressed against the glove compartment. It's hard to tell how much it's my sister and how much it's the medicine to blame (my father talked her into taking her pills again).

My mother drives cautiously up the narrow, winding roads of Coldwater Canyon. She glances back at me in the rearview mirror and wonders if it's too much air. Should she roll up the window a bit? The way she asks it makes Cora turn around to look at me. But my sister doesn't stop rattling off which celebrity homes have burned to the ground recently.

"Every year it's the same thing," she says, and then waves her hand out the window at some producer's place. "He did *Spartacus*.

It's just whichever way the wind's blowing. Everybody's out by their swimming pools holding a hose, waiting to see if they're—"

My mother takes one hand from the steering wheel and pats my sister on the arm.

"Why don't we just enjoy the scenery for a few minutes?" she says.

Cora stops drumming her fingers on the roof and peers back over her shoulder at me. "Christ," she says. "Mr. Sensitive."

We're up pretty high now and you can see the city, its lights sparkling like a runway below us.

But then suddenly the station wagon jerks like a bumper car.

"Something's wrong, Teddy," my mother says. "It's not doing anything. I've got my foot all the way down on the accelerator."

"We're going backward," Cora says, her eyes wide. "We're going the other way."

"My foot's on the floor," my mother pleads.

I reach over her shoulder to help steer us onto the side of the road.

"Set the emergency brake," I say as soon as we come to a stop.

"Oh, Lord," my mother says. She lowers her forehead to the steering wheel. "I thought it was me. I thought I wasn't feeling anything in my legs."

But we're just out of gas. The needle is in the red.

"I thought he's supposed to be the man of the house now," my sister says, hiking her thumb back at me. "So how come he doesn't take care of the damn car?"

"All right," my mother says. "I don't want to hear any of it. Just lock your doors and keep the windows up."

Everyone is quiet for a moment, even Cora, and you can hear the cicadas outside hissing in the dry brush. Then my sister remembers reading how they found some starlet's body near here.

"Right off Mulholland," she says. "It couldn't be more than a half mile over—"

"Honest to God, Cora," my mother snaps, twisting her hands on the steering wheel. "Will you just be quiet this once? I swear to God."

I lean against the door and after a while try to think about

Panama. One other thing I remember about the Darien jungle was how the children in the tribes there never cried. The person who wrote the book thought it was because the Indians didn't really seem to get attached to anyone, not even to members of their own family. After every place the author had been in that country, he still thought it was the strangest thing he'd ever seen.

Up ahead a house on piers juts out from the side of the mountain. The windows must be twenty feet high and I wonder if it's ever had to be rebuilt. It's so big, it could belong to anyone, and I try to imagine myself standing in the living room gazing down at my mother and sister in their stalled car beside the road. I'm older, as old as my father, and rich enough that I'd never have to worry about a brushfire burning everything to the ground. If I wanted to I'd just build it all back up the next year. Or if I changed my mind I could move to someplace like Panama and stay there as long as I wanted, but it wouldn't really matter since no one would be waiting for me back in the States.

PARIS
of the
ORIENT

My father returned from Vietnam in no mood to hear about his second cousin twice removed. But Cora has finally tracked down the former child actor who was once under contract with MGM. Only, my father will have nothing to do with her proposed family reunion and spends most of his first week home up in the attic packing for our next assignment. We are off to Ft. Polk—everyone, that is, except Cora, who will start back to college the end of the month.

"I mean, when's he going to come down to earth?" my exasperated sister says as my father's footsteps thump overhead.

"Try to remember where your father's been," my mother reminds her. After Panama my father volunteered for Vietnam. "Just give him a little time."

But both Cora and I have seen *The Green Berets* and for once I have to agree with my sister. Whatever my father is suffering from, it isn't shell shock.

By Friday, Cora decides on a different tack. She's studying film at UCLA, isn't she? Then who better to get to know than a relative practically born in the business?

"The man's a producer," she tries out at breakfast. "Think of the people he must know. What do you think? Lucy Arnaz made it on raw talent alone?"

But my father isn't about to impose on a complete stranger.

"We played with each other a couple times when were were kids.

69

Way before his mother took him out to Hollywood. I wouldn't recognize the man today if he walked through that damn door." And he points with his fork. "So your answer is no. I'm not having us barge in on anybody I don't know from Adam."

Just the day before, my sister's thyroid erupted again. Now she touches her swollen throat and I know she's going to pull out all the stops. As a family we must seem relentless to my father. My mother bitterly resents his spending so many years overseas. Nor is she any happier about having to leave Cora behind while the rest of us set off for some outpost in the Deep South. After being passed over for promotion for the first time in his career, my father volunteered for combat. Yet even I feel cheated by his listlessness. Who else, after all, is he supposed to get excited about seeing than his own family?

Later, having emptied the attic, my father descends to the greater challenge of the basement. But when he starts carting up Cora's mammoth collection of movie magazines, my sister rushes down from her room breathless and infuriated.

"They're going with me," she insists. "I'm taking them to school."

My father toes one of the bulging boxes. "Used to be they had you read books in college."

My sister, who never cries, is very nearly in tears. "You come back here like you're Sam Goldwyn or something," she says, her shoulders trembling. "Well, you're not. You're not even a star."

My father appears dumbstruck.

"That's enough of that kind of talk," my mother says.

But Cora's hyperthyroid eyes are popping. "Maybe I should just go out and rip up all his ridiculous tomato plants," she says. "See how he likes it."

My father slides the box into the corner, then looks up. "That'll do," he says.

And Cora knows from his tone that it will. For a moment I have to read lips to follow anything. The blood is pounding in my ears. My father hasn't been back ten minutes and already everybody is at each other's throat.

That night, in bed, I listen to him try to get my mother to keep her voice down. But except for when she hisses the word *geisha* so that it sounds like a threat, not much is new. When, at last, their light goes out, I put my hand on my chest and feel my heart pumping crazily. This is when I like to think about gurus. About how they can make their pulse slow down by falling into a certain trance. But it's impossible for me to imagine ever being able to think like a swami. Especially with my family.

The following morning my father is out in the yard digging up his tomato plants. Whenever he's home on leave, it's all he seems to tend to. Somehow a few have managed to endure his long absences. Now he wants me to see if a couple of the hardier ones might survive a week in a U-Haul.

"Kind of a rough night," I say, watching him aerate the soil with a trowel.

He looks up at me blankly. "You mean your sister?"

It turns out that Cora had been sick.

"You saw her throw up?" I say skeptically.

My father crawls on his hands and knees to the next plant. Fingering its weak stem, he decides it's too fragile for the move and passes it up. I can see how his hair is thinning on top. He's getting older, something more noticeable to me after not seeing him for so long.

"She doesn't take her pills," he says, flicking the dirt from his fingers, "and then she wonders why she gets nauseous."

I sit on the edge of the stone patio as he considers whether the leaf rot looks fatal. Something is definitely different about my father. He's become preoccupied, abstracted, like a boarder eager to move on. And it strikes me that whatever this house is for the rest of us, it's never been home for him.

"So what's it like over there?" I ask, stretching my legs out on the warm stones. "I mean, when they're not shooting at each other."

My father wipes his hands on his khaki pants and leans back on one elbow. I can see from his sunny expression that just the thought of the place relaxes him.

"Remarkably practical people. Humble. Straightforward. Not a

sneaky bone in their body. Things you just don't see much of back
here."

"Pearl Harbor wasn't sneaky?" I'm jealous of my father's affection.
I want it all for myself, not squandered on foreigners.

"Wrong country," he says.

"You mean if you've seen one you haven't seen them all?"

He's heard this sort of thing from Cora but seems surprised to
hear it from me.

"If they're such paragons," I say, "how come they can't even live
together? I mean, they're not even one country?"

When he stands up, the joints of his ankles crack.

"Got me there," my father says, peeling his damp T-shirt over his
head.

His chest is pale, the tanned line of his arms like a paper-doll
cutout. And I feel a sudden rush of remorse. He has enough trouble
with Cora and my mother without having to put up with my
carping.

"You need some help with the basement?" I offer.

He twists his T-shirt over one of the tied-up tomato plants, the
sweat coiling out.

"It's a miracle the junk down there hasn't spontaneously com-
busted by now," he says. "Sometime when you were all asleep."

"Mom's up half the night whenever you're away."

My father gazes at the chain link fence that separates the yard
from our neighbor's.

"Your mother wouldn't go to the pound with me. If she'd put a
damn dog out here the way I tried to get her to, she might get to
bed at a decent hour."

"You know Mom," I say.

My father wraps the damp shirt around his neck. "That's the
problem."

"What do you think?" Cora says, peering over my shoulder at the
bathroom mirror. "Are they puffy?

It's the second time she's asked me in the last hour. My sister is
anxious about meeting my father's cousin.

"Trust me," I say, drawing the razor across my smooth jaw. Several new whiskers have sprouted on my chin, and to show off, I've left the door open. "They're as ugly as they've always been. Nothing's changed."

She continues to study herself in the mirror. "I can't get an honest answer out of anyone in this family. Mom lies through her teeth, and Daddy pretends not to know what I'm even talking about. But I can see for myself. I look like Peter Lorre. I'm not blind."

I bend over and splash water in my face. "You keep looking long enough," I say, "you're going to see whatever you want to see."

"I look like a goddamn bat," and she presses down gingerly on one eyelid. "It's not fair," she says, catching me staring at her the wrong way. "I had eyes like Liz."

When my sister isn't driving me crazy, I manage to feel sorry for her. It *does* seem unfair. People always said she had beautiful eyes. Something they don't say anymore.

My mother stops me in the hall. "Look at this," she says, lifting my chin. I stuck a piece of toilet paper to a nick. "You have no business with a razor in your hand. Now, I don't want to see you carving up your face again."

Downstairs, my father is already dressed, rereading the thick letter from one of his former Vietnamese counterparts. He spent most of the afternoon grousing, until my mother put her foot down.

"So what's your pen pal got to say?" I ask.

Before he can fold the letter back up, I see his name printed across the top in a childlike scrawl.

"Worrying about the kids mostly."

"I thought they were supposed to honor their parents so much."

My father pulls the car keys from his pocket. "They're all watching American TV now. The youngest one wants her eyes less slanty."

Cora, who inherited her radar ears from my mother, suddenly saunters in from the kitchen. "She can have mine," she says. "My compliments."

"*Gunsmoke*'s a big hit," my father says. "Somehow they pick up the satellite feed from France."

Cora laughs. "I can just see it," she says. "Festus ordering a shot of rotgut. *'Donnez-moi un Dubonnet.'*"

When my mother comes down, I can tell that she expects my father to say something about her outfit. She's spent almost as much time as Cora getting ready. But my father only sulks out the door to the carport.

"Like an hour out of his life is such a big deal," my sister says.

"I wouldn't press your luck with your father right now," my mother says. "I really wouldn't."

"Give me a break," Cora says. "It's his own damn cousin, for cryin' out loud."

"Second cousin," I say, scratching the tissue paper from my chin. "Twice removed."

They both look over at me as if one of the house plants just talked.

"Does he really have to go?" my sister says. "I mean, what if it calls for adult conversation?"

"I'm warning you two," my mother says. "Your father's not in the best frame of mind for this."

In fact, we're barely out of the driveway before he glances murderously into the rearview mirror.

"His mother knew my mother," he says. "That was the extent of—"

"Why don't we just enjoy the scenery," my mother says. "It's a lovely sunset."

And it is: a great big orange volleyball sinking into the ocean beyond Santa Monica. As we rise into the tortuous Hollywood Hills, the thick palm and banana trees hide many of the houses set back from the narrow streets. Heeding my mother's advice, Cora dispenses with her usual travelogue.

But as we come up Mulholland Drive less than a block from the address, my sister lurches forward, pointing like a gundog.

"Look!"

I turn to see someone shooting baskets in a driveway.

"Didn't you recognize him?" Cora says, beaming excitedly. "*My Three Sons*? Tim Considine?"

She'd spun around in her seat as we passed, shaking her head in disbelief. But none of us really got a good look.

At the corner my mother nods at a disappointingly plain, ranch-style house that could fit into any middle-class suburb.

"That's it there," she says, having already scouted out the neighborhood with Cora.

My father pulls over, the hubcaps scraping against the curb. He turns off the engine and glares at the rearview mirror.

"One drink and we're out of here."

Cora has flipped open her compact and is squinting at herself. "Daddy, I don't see why—"

"Sixty minutes," he says. "End of discussion."

We follow him up the brick walkway to the porch while my sister explains to the rest of us why the really powerful people in show business prefer to live inconspicuously.

"They don't want a lot of hoopla in their everyday lives. They get enough of that in—"

"I'm going to knock on the door," my father says. "Are we ready to calm down here?"

My mother smiles at my sister. "I know you're excited, sweetheart. But let's just see if we can take it a little slower."

Cora is on her tiptoes, craning to see if Tim Considine is still in the driveway when the door eases open and a tall Oriental woman peers out at us. It's obvious that she has no idea who we are.

"Is Mr. Kelly in?" my father says.

Cora steps forward. "He's expecting us. I talked to him on the phone. A couple times."

The woman closes her eyes, shaking her head. "Of course. Of course." There's not a trace of an accent. "I'm so sorry. Jimmy's so forgetful. He's over on the tennis courts. Come in. Come in." And she bumps the door open with her hip. "He shouts a dozen things at me before he flies out of the house. He just went to hit a few balls. He should be back any minute."

She's too casually dressed for a domestic (white shorts and a halter top), and I can see my mother already sizing her up. As she sizes up every younger woman in my father's company. But coincidentally Susie is from Sasebo, Japan. A city my father once refueled in.

While our hostess fixes gin and tonics, Cora points out the signed pictures of celebrities on the piano. But neither my mother nor I can take our eyes off the life-size, full-frontal nude oil painting over the fireplace.

"Jimmy's second wife," Susie says when she catches us gaping. She sets the tray of drinks down on the glass coffee table. "A very talented off-Broadway actress."

"And you're Mrs. Kelly?" my mother says.

Susie glances in my general direction. "His houseguest," she says cheerfully. "Jimmy and I met in Tokyo. He was working with the Ice Capades. And there I was."

"In the show?" Cora says.

Susie wipes the bottom of her glass across her bare forearm. "Strange as it seems."

"Then you're a professional skater?" my father says.

"Oh, a few years back. I actually learned in Rockefeller Center, believe it or not."

I can tell from my mother's expression that she doesn't.

"I wasn't as good as most of the girls," she says. "But then most of the girls couldn't speak Japanese."

"It must have helped," my father says. His mood has improved considerably.

"I wound up a kind of union representative. Which was good because I broke my leg two days into the show. And Jimmy just sort of took me under his wing."

My father and I can't help glancing at her shapely legs. They're tanned and long and show no sign of any injury.

Later, after several uneasy lulls in the conversation, a small, wiry, remarkably freckled man bounds in the front door with a tennis racket at his hip.

"Fuck," he says, wrapping his arm around my father's shoulder. "I'm late." Then, seeing me, he covers his eyes comically.

My mother swirls her gin and tonic with her finger. "He's heard worse."

When everyone turns expectantly toward me, I nod in agreement. "Mostly from my sister."

Jimmy spears his tennis racket in the brass umbrella stand and bursts out laughing. "So this is my pen pal," he says, winking at Cora. "Jesus, Susie, look at this knockout."

And even I have to admit that my sister looks good. But then over the years she's probably picked up more beauty tips from the stars than anyone alive. Cora spent most of the day trying to conceal the effects of her condition. A high collar and scarf cover up her throat, but there's no way to hide her eyes.

"Lovely," Susie says. She's retreated politely from the conversation, standing back, content to agree with whatever Jimmy asks. This is perhaps just the sort of humility my father was talking about. And the reason he suddenly seems so much at home.

Jimmy sits down next to Cora on the leather couch and pats her knee. My sister doesn't like to be touched but she is also a very good actress.

"Absolutely incredible, her take on this town," he says. He's still sweating from the tennis and runs his fingers through his damp hair. "It's like I'm talking to some talent agent fifty years in the business. I say to Susie she's a fucking . . . she's like this Hollywood almanac. Am I right, honey?"

Susie nods at the rest of us. "It's exactly what he said."

My mother guzzles her gin and tonic as if she's been the one out on the courts. I can see that she'd be happy to keep our visit to the quick drink my father insisted on. But Jimmy has already whisked him out to the pool to reminisce about their lost childhood in upstate New York.

Susie, again thrust into the role of hostess, can only ply my mother with more gin and tonics, and my sister and me with one of Jimmy's early scrapbooks.

"I see you're neighbors with Tim Considine," Cora volunteers when my mother makes no effort to be sociable.

Susie bends another plastic tray of ice cubes over the pitcher. "Jimmy's right," she says. "You really *don't* miss anything." And with no one else seeming to pay any attention to her, she smiles at me. "Tim pretty much likes to keep to himself."

I know even before she looks up from the album how my sister is going to take this.

"You don't have to worry," Cora says, smoothing out a clipping of Jimmy in some Broadway musical. "I'm not interested in autographs."

Susie shakes her head. "Oh, I didn't mean—"

But my father suddenly steps back in from the patio.

"I ought to put this guy on the payroll," Jimmy says to my mother.

Cora's ears prick up.

"Jimmy's thinking about doing something on Ho Chi Minh City," Susie says.

My mother holds her palm up like a traffic cop. "Well, he ought to know that neck of the woods by now."

"Look at this," Cora says. She turns the thick album for the rest of us to see. There's a photograph of Jimmy as a teenager sitting next to Liz Taylor when she was in *National Velvet*.

"A publicity still," Jimmy says dismissively. "Everyone under contract had their picture taken with her. The poor kid. There was enough envy coming from the rest of the studio brats to light Warners."

"But you knew her?" Cora says.

"We were supposed to be one big happy family," Jimmy says. "We weren't. We were a bunch of—little egos. It's boring, really." He looks over at Susie. "We got swimsuits for this crowd? I need a dip. I've been sweating like a pig." He stands beside my father as if to compare physiques. "Mine'll be a little loose on you. That's not a married man's gut. You working out?"

My father avoids my mother's eyes. "Just clean living."

After outfitting my sister, Susie finds a pair of large boxer trunks for me.

"My son wears these when he visits," she says, and then smiles when she holds them up. "You're built like your father."

Outside, I pad barefoot across the redwood deck, a towel wrapped around my waist. My father is standing in the shallow end of the pool.

"It was the Paris of the Orient," Jimmy is saying to him. "What we've done to that city's criminal."

My father listens solemnly, arms crossed at his chest. It's hard to tell if Jimmy is trying to start an argument with him. My father is the least political man I know.

My mother sits on one of the chaise lounges, her feet up and her shoes off. She's still in her clothes.

"I didn't know you liked gin and tonics that much," I say to her.

"What do you think, sweetheart? Your mother needs to lose a little weight?" She wasn't able to fit into any of the swimsuits. "Your sister says it's what keeps daddies down on the farm."

She gazes past me, and I turn to see Cora and then Susie come out through the sliding glass door. As my sister walks toward us, she rolls her eyes. Susie has on a spectacularly revealing bikini (from Ice Capades?). It's a solid caramel color and I have to squint. She'd stepped over to the ladder, and with her back to us I thought at first that she wasn't wearing anything.

Cora sets her towel down. "That ought to shake up the troops."

She means, of course, to goad my suspicious mother. It doesn't help that Susie is both attractive and Oriental. While my father fought one war overseas, my mother was waging another at home. His absence has not made her heart grow any fonder. Only xenophobic.

"It doesn't surprise me," she says under her breath. "In the least."

My father scoops water over his shoulders to try to appear indifferent. He knows that my jealous mother is watching his every move.

"Let's go," Jimmy shouts, waving to the rest of us. "Everybody in the pool."

My suit hangs too low on me, and Cora grins when I stand up. She has on a simple maillot that fits her better than her own. I can tell that she thinks it's flattering.

Diving into the deep end, I have to grab my trunks as I come up.

Cora walks around the pool and sits down in front of me, dipping her toes in the water.

"Quite a bod the girl's got," she whispers. Susie is sitting cross-legged on the wooden deck trying to pin her hair up. "Bet she keeps the old boy's skates sharp."

"Why don't you get off Mom's case," I say. "She doesn't need you telling her she's fat."

My sister only shrugs her shoulders. "Hey, just some daughterly advice."

More than once during the next hour I try to catch my father's eye. I'm not interested in poring over any more Hollywood scrapbooks with Cora. Or in listening to Jimmy's complaints about Vietnamese bureaucrats. ("Everything has to be done behind someone's back. It's a way of life over there.") I don't care about Vietnam. All I want is for the war to be over between my mother and father.

As it gets darker, Susie lights the kerosene torches around the pool, and the water shines in brilliant strips of turquoise.

"Actually," my sister says, watching Susie stretch back out on her towel, "she's not all that bad. If you can look past the exhibitionism. As I know you can."

"I think Mom's looped," I say. "That's about five gin and tonics."

Cora yawns. "On the other hand, Jimmy's a jerk."

For some reason my father's cousin hasn't lived up to her expectations. I'm not sure why, exactly. Other than that my sister has a habit of always building things up in her head.

Susie has brought out the box of cigars Jimmy asked her for, and when she leans over the edge of the pool with the lighter, the top of her swimsuit droops open.

"Now, *that's* a smoke," Cora whispers.

Jimmy raises one of the cigars for my mother to see. "Cuban," he calls out. "All the way from Hong Kong."

From the other end of the deck my mother lifts her glass as if in a toast. "Better watch your friend there. He's not used to them."

My father grins sheepishly.

"No problem," Jimmy says, encouraged that my mother seems to be warming to him. "We know CPR here."

Susie only occasionally tiptoes up to my mother with a bowl of macadamia nuts (declined) or the fortune cookies from Jimmy's own homemade recipe.

I smile at my sister, pleased to know something she doesn't. "Guess who has a kid as old as you?" I say.

Cora flips her wet hair straight back. "Let me guess. Is he bigger than a bread box?" She speaks out of the corner of her mouth like a cabdriver. My father and Jimmy aren't that far away. "Does he have great big shoulders too?"

"What's so funny?"

My sister holds on to the side of the pool and flutter-kicks her legs a few times. "My, what big shorts you have on." And she laughs. "You really are priceless."

I don't want to listen to whose swimsuit she thinks it actually is. It would only be some crackpot idea she's come up with. "Let *me* guess," I say, looking out at Susie, who's standing between my father and Jimmy in the water. "Tim Considine's really *her* third son."

I don't know whether it's the chlorine or her medicine that makes my sister's eyes glisten. But for a second I think that this is what a crazy person looks like.

"Very good," she says. "And just when I was about to give up on my little brother."

I pull myself out of the pool, tugging my swimsuit back up on my hips. "And I guess the letters Dad gets aren't really from who he says they're from, right?"

She only tilts her head as if there's water in her ear.

"Everything has to be some kind of Hollywood plot with you," I say. "You live in a dreamworld."

My mother smiles dimly at me as I come over to her.

"My boy's getting so big," she says. "He's not my baby anymore."

I sit down on the other folding chair. "Tell that to Cora."

When she reaches for the towel to wrap around my shoulders, the empty pitcher shatters on the deck.

"Nobody move," Susie says. She's already up, prying her sandals on. "I'm an old hand at this."

My mother doesn't seem at all embarrassed and so I know that she's drunk. While our hostess bends nimbly at the waist, poking the broom under the chaise lounge, my mother keeps her bare feet up.

I look over Susie's backside at my sister, who puckers her lips and blows a kiss back at me.

"Time to go," my mother says, and stands up, her arms out like a tightrope walker's.

Jimmy objects only halfheartedly, and my father comes up the pool steps slowly, looking a little peaked from the cigar.

I follow my mother into the house and wait outside the bathroom with my ear to the door. "I'm going down the hall to take off my suit now," I say.

After a while I hear her clear her throat. "Fine, honey," she says weakly. "You do that."

Jimmy has drawn my father into the den to show him a few last mementos from his Far East travels. Cora, meanwhile, changes quickly and wanders out the front door to avoid Susie, who's wrapping up the leftover fortune cookies for us.

I hang my suit on the shower rod and then open the medicine cabinet above the sink. Except for a razor and a can of shaving cream, it's empty. I examine my chin in the mirror and don't know what to be more depressed about: snooping or taking my sister seriously.

Cora has opened the back of the station wagon when the rest of us emerge from the house together. She lowers the tailgate with a curious half-mocking expression. She's been up to something but I don't know what. We all shake hands and promise to get together again, which only my father probably thinks is possible.

Susie, wearing a man's terry cloth robe, waves bravely at us. The robe, I notice, is several sizes too big. Jimmy stands beside her puffing away on a new cigar.

"Mr. and Mrs. Sonja Henie at home," Cora says, rolling her window back up. She seems a little out of breath, as if she's just run around the block.

My father isn't a smoker, and as he steers the station wagon down through the steep hills, the back of his neck grows damp and clammy, until my mother, doubled over beside him from all the twisting and turning, raps the dashboard with her knuckles to stop the car.

"You all right?" my father asks her.

"Just pull over."

It's pitch dark out as the tires crunch on the gravel shoulder of the road. My father sets the brake and comes around the front of the car to unlock my mother's door.

"You need to be sick?" he says, ducking in, his grim face only inches from hers.

I watch them hobble together down the shallow embankment, where my mother drops to her knees like a penitent in the singed grass.

"Pathetic," Cora says, glaring out her window at them.

We listen to my mother heaving her gin and tonics in the ditch.

"Why don't you cut them a little slack," I say angrily. "They're having a hard time of it right now. Can't you see that?"

The whites of my sister's eyes flash in the dark, and for a moment I half expect her to lunge at me in the backseat.

"*They're* having a hard time of it! *They're* having a hard time of it!" She unravels the silk scarf from her throat. "And who do you think caused this?"

She's convinced herself that her condition was brought on by stress.

I look out at my father, slumped beside my mother as if joining her in prayer. "Probably them."

Stunned by my concession, my sister can only nod, mumbling under her breath, "That's right."

I don't want to argue and instead hold out the bag of fortune cookies, which seems to calm her down.

"Mom ought to get a boyfriend," she says finally. "That'd settle his hash."

I open my own door. "Somebody's liable to come around that curve too fast to stop."

My sister slides across the seat after me. "Hold on a minute. I got a little souvenir for you."

I start walking backward up the hill as she reaches in to pull something out of the rear of the station wagon.

"Amuse yourself," Cora shouts, and then flings a basketball that bounces once on the macadam before rolling off the side of the road.

I come back and pick it up.

"There it was, just sitting in the driveway," my sister says. "And Tim nowhere to be found for an autograph."

I can hear my mother still retching in the dark. "You're crazy," I say, tucking the basketball under my arm. "You're all crazy."

A van strains up the hill, the driver flicking his brights on when he sees us. But it's traffic coming the other way that worries me. I turn and trot far enough up the road, where I can at least flag anyone down in time.

Sitting on one of the guard-rail stumps, I try to catch my breath. Below me the city sparkles like the stars used to in the desert.

I press my fingertips to my neck and feel my pulse still throbbing wildly. From the crumbled cookie in my pants pocket I pull the small tape out and try to read my fortune in the moonlight. My sister is right. There's nothing inscrutable about my future the way I'm going. I'm headed for an ulcer before I have a driver's license. Only, what else am I supposed to do? Let some semi plow into the station wagon? I'm almost bitter enough to look the other way. To let them suffer whatever fate comes barreling around the bend. But of course I don't. In a few more minutes my mother will be able to crawl back into the car and we'll all be on our way again.

I set the basketball down and try to remember which of the three sons was Tim Considine. I never really watched the show that much in reruns. Mostly because every week one of the boys would get into trouble that was pretty trivial when the biggest trouble of all no one ever seemed to mention. What bothered me so much was how they kept pretending to be one big happy family. But how could they be, really? They didn't even have both parents. And how was anything supposed to be funny after that?

THE HOMEFRONT

"And the puffiness?" my mother asks. She stands beside Cora's hospital bed, anxiously twisting the corner of the starched sheet.

"That's something that's hard to predict," the captain says.

What was less difficult to predict was that my sister would fall in love with her bachelor physician.

"But it should start to go down?" my mother says.

Cora sits up in the elevated bed. She is sensitive about her protruding eyes. She doesn't want them talked about in front of her leading man.

"There'll be a pencil-thin incision," the doctor says, drawing an imaginary line across my sister's neck, "which should heal nicely. With a little sun it'll hardly be noticeable."

I can see Cora smile at the thought of basking on the beach at Grand Isle with her favorite army physician. But I notice that the captain avoids saying anything about what a little sun will do for her eyes.

"And the swollenness?" my mother persists, gently tracing Cora's brow with her finger.

My sister ducks away from my mother's hand. "If it doesn't bother me, why does it bother you so much?"

But my mother only wants her daughter's best feature, her large, lovely eyes, back to normal.

"Let's just see how it goes," my father says. He's as eager as Cora for her to be able to get back to school in the fall. She has been a difficult patient. But by having it done here at Ft. Polk during the summer, the army will pay for everything. A civilian hospital on the West Coast would have cost a fortune.

"Undoubtedly best," the captain says, relieved not to come between his commanding officer's wife and petulant daughter. "I think we're all going to be happy with the results."

My mother nods confidently. "She'll thank me later."

"Thank you for what?" Cora says. She shifts against the stacked pillows at her back. "What're you, assisting in the operation?"

One of the classic symptoms of my sister's condition is a general edginess, a hypersensitivity. With Cora, of course, it's hard to know when it's her thyroid and when it's just her prickly personality.

Still, it isn't a simple procedure even for an accomplished surgeon. But I know better than to ask upsetting questions in front of my sister the day before her operation.

"You're my daughter," my mother says. "I want to know what's being done for you. That's my responsibility."

A nurse sticks her head in the door and smiles at the captain. "Call on seven, doctor. You can take it in the hall."

He steps around my mother to squeeze Cora's shoulder affectionately. "Can't wait to get my hands on this young lady's throat," and he winks at my father, who lowers his *Army Times*.

"Thanks for everything, Doc."

My sister winces. I wave good-bye. And my mother eyes the attractive nurse suspiciously.

"Who's hungry?" my father says as soon as the door swings shut. "How about some takeout?"

Cora has already had a salad prepared by the dietician.

"Nothing for me," my mother says.

But the point is to get her out of the room for a while. Cora is ready to pounce on the next word my mother utters.

"You keep the patient entertained," my father says, steering my mother past me and into the hall. "We'll bring you something."

As soon as they are gone, Cora presses her fists to her temple. "That woman drives me absolutely bananas."

"She's just nervous," I offer, unzipping my backpack. "You know how she is about hospitals."

"I don't care about how she is," my sister says bitterly. "*I'm* the patient. *Me.* Can't she get that through her thick skull?"

Cora blames my mother for putting her here. She's persuaded that her goiter is the result of unreasonable pressures put upon her. I don't know exactly what pressures she believes my mother has exerted, but I decide against asking. As my sister's thyroid has enlarged these past few months, so has her general hostility toward my mother. The tension between them has driven my father on repeated out-of-state inspections.

I reach into my backpack. This girl I've been seeing, Patricia, will be seventeen on Saturday and I found an antique perfume bottle in the thrift shop run by the Officers' Wives Auxiliary. The silver top had to be replated, which wound up costing more than the bottle had originally, but it came out beautifully and I want to show it off to Cora.

Lifting the lid from the box, I set the bottle down on the bed stand. "What do you think?"

My sister looks curiously at me for a moment and then picks it up, examining its markings and the sunburst design in the crystal. "I probably won't die, you know? I mean, people survive this all the time."

"What?"

She is suddenly blinking rapidly. "It's not that big a deal."

But I don't know what she's talking about.

"I've got the best surgeon in the army," she says.

I start to reach down for the perfume bottle but catch myself.

"It was a very sweet thing to do," my sister says, and sets it in her lap. "And very uncharacteristic."

I nod gloomily.

"You had the top redone," she says. "That must have cost you."

I run the tip of my tongue along the back of my teeth. The ridge is like a miniature mountain range and I bite down until it stings.

"They did a nice job," Cora concedes, squinting appraisingly at the Art Nouveau design. "But for future reference, you don't want to alter an antique. It takes away from its value." She places the perfume bottle back down on the nightstand and checks the *TV Guide*. "*On the Beach* is on at eight," she says. "Tony Perkins with an Australian accent. Great casting."

But I'm trying to think of what else I can come up with for a present by Saturday.

". . . a captain," Cora is saying, aiming the remote control at the television. "The man's a god. And single. How is it humanly possible?"

I consider stealing the bottle back and letting her think that someone has taken it.

Of course I'm glad that my sister has such faith in her doctor, but even she has to doubt that the effects of her condition are completely reversible. I want to say something about my tongue being pretty much back to normal but think better of it. It still looks a little mangled, but at least I can keep my mouth shut. Which this time, at least, I manage to do.

My parents come back with Chinese, and Cora watches sullenly as we eat. She isn't allowed anything until morning.

Afterward, she falls asleep while my mother and I sit through the rest of the movie. My father has gone down to the lobby to finish a letter to one of his Vietnamese buddies.

"I don't want to watch the ending if it's going to be sad," my mother whispers. "You think it's going to be sad, honey?"

I look over at her. The entire human race has been obliterated by a nuclear war. And now Tony Perkins and his wife are about to kill themselves after just having put their baby out of its misery.

"It doesn't look real promising, Mom."

"Let's turn it off, then."

But I know that she won't let me.

"Why does Hollywood have to be so negative?" my mother says, keeping her voice down. "When I was growing up you could still go to the movies and be entertained. Now it's all gloom and doom."

"Maybe because there's a lot of it around," I say.

We watch Perkins swallow the last cyanide pill.

"I don't see why he has to do that," she says.

"What's the alternative?" I say. "He's going to be breathing radioactive dust here any minute."

"You always have a choice," my mother insists. "Don't let anyone tell you different."

It's the kind of conversation I could only have with my mother. I've tried to persuade her, as long as she's here, to have a few tests run on her legs, which continue to give her trouble, but all she wants to worry about right now, she says, is Cora. And so we both watch the young naval lieutenant lie down beside his dead wife and close his eyes. The first time I saw the movie with Cora I had to struggle to keep from blubbering. My sister had seemed unmoved. "Perkins just doesn't do it for me," she said as the lights came on in the post theater. But the truth is my sister takes after my stoic father.

My mother wipes her nose with one of the paper napkins from the Nankin Inn.

"I don't know what the point is," she says, shaking her head at the television as the credits roll against the ocean's backdrop. "Why do they show stuff like that? Just to upset people? Aren't there enough terrible things going on that they don't have to make movies about them?"

"It's supposed to make you think," I say.

My mother stands up, wincing from the pain in her leg muscles. "I want to be entertained. I don't want to have to think. I have enough to think about already."

"Well," I say, "it's a pretty important subject. I mean, look what can happen."

"I already know what can happen. It doesn't take a genius to figure that out."

"Maybe it's a good idea to remind ourselves."

"That's why we elect a president." She pulls the blanket up over my sister's shoulder. "So *he* can remind himself."

I laugh mockingly. Not for anything she's said but because I suddenly want to blame her for Cora's condition too.

"You'd rather pass the buck," I say, "instead of facing the truth and trying to do something about it."

When she turns around, her brow is creased as if she's trying hard to figure out what I'm talking about.

"I'm just one person," she says, and lowers her voice when my sister stirs. "Who cares what your mother thinks? What difference is that going to make?"

"You elected the president, didn't you?"

She smiles sadly at me. "I didn't vote, sweetheart. Your father was out of the country. I never got down to the firehouse to register."

In her sleep my sister's eyes look like poached eggs. I'm nervous about the operation. I've read too much about what can go wrong.

"That's typical," I say, and my mother waves her hand for me to keep my voice down. "I mean, aren't we supposed to be citizens of this country? Okay, we're a family. You're my mother. She's my sister. And Dad's down in the lobby. But we're Americans too. That's what a democracy's about. Only, nobody in this family even takes the time to vote."

My mother stops nodding.

"You're right, sweetheart." She suddenly looks tired and defeated. As if my civics lesson has summed up all her failings. "I don't do my share. I'm too caught up in our own little world to think about the bigger one the way I should. That's why I'm sending you and your sister to college. So you can make up for your uneducated mother."

It's useless to argue.

"I guess I'll get a ride from Dad," I say. "I can still make the last half of class." I've started taking karate lessons.

"He's probably fallen asleep." My mother spreads the sheet over the couch and tucks it under the cushions. "He likes the chairs down there."

I swing my backpack over my shoulder, glancing at the perfume bottle on my sister's bedstand.

"I don't think your father slept well last night either," my mother says.

With the television off there's only the light from the small bed lamp. My mother changes into her pajamas in the bathroom. She'll spend the night on the narrow couch to be with Cora.

"Your sister's going to be fine," she says when I apologize for arguing with her. "That's all that matters."

And when I look at Cora in the raised hospital bed, her throat swollen and her closed eyes twitching, I think that my mother is right. What *does* it matter if the world blows up tomorrow? As long as my sister is going to be fine.

"I want you to be careful with all that punching stuff," my mother says. "I don't need two of you in the hospital."

I find my father slumped over in one of the plastic chairs in the empty waiting room.

"Dad?"

He opens one eye.

"Mom's gone to bed," I say. "You think you could drop me off at class?"

He exhales heavily. "Your mother's going to put her legs out of commission on that damn couch."

He doesn't see the point of her spending the night again. Cora's medication will keep her out until morning.

"But that's your mother," he says, patting his pocket for the keys. "You want to drive?"

In the car we keep the windows open, which makes it difficult to hear each other.

"Your sister's going to do great," my father says, raising his voice. "I'm not worried about her. It's your mother should be seeing someone."

I nod. "It's like pulling teeth."

My father doesn't look over at me. We've had this conversation before. "This is true."

The dojo is on the second floor of one of the old war barracks that's been converted into a teen center for dependents.

My father slides over into the driver's seat when I get out.

"I guess I'll call if I can't get a lift," I say.

He readjusts the rearview mirror. All he seems to do is chauffeur the rest of us. He is as eager for me to get my own license as my mother is reluctant.

After three months of classes two nights a week, I am still only a white belt. Our instructor, a staff sergeant with tattoos of dragons on his forearms, doesn't believe in early promotion.

I quickly change into my *ghi*, taking my place in the back row. Beneath the thick cotton uniform sweat starts to trickle down from under my arms, even though I've missed the strenuous warm-up.

The rest of the hour we are paired off for arm and leg pounding, a painful exercise of beating on each other's limbs to harden our bodies. I've taken to wearing long-sleeve shirts even in the dead of summer to conceal the bruises. The first welt my mother spotted would have ended any more arm and leg pounding. Not to mention the sergeant's having to explain his regimen to the MPs. If Patricia hadn't been paired off with me that first night, I doubt I would have come back for more.

After class I meet her on the street. She has her own car, a convertible she bought from her stepfather, a warrant officer who my father describes as a "head case."

"We'll stop by my place," she says. "I want to get out of this stuff."

She has on a T-shirt beneath her *ghi*. It's soaked to the skin.

The only time I've brought her by the house, she wasn't wearing a bra and I never heard the end of it. "Kind of thing to cause a stampede," Cora said to me later. "If you're a steer." My mother had simply remarked that she hoped her only son could do better than that. "Got to believe," my sister said.

"I guess this operation's got everybody spooked," Patricia says. The top is down on the convertible and she climbs into the driver's seat without opening the door. "Whatever you do, don't get my old lady started on surgery. She's had one of everything taken out."

When she stops at the gas station right outside the gates, I walk over to the pay phone and call my father.

"I'll leave the door unlocked" is all he says when I tell him I don't need a ride.

Patricia had pulled up to a self-service pump but the attendant has come out anyway. He's stocky and appears to be something of a body builder.

"Hey, lady," he is saying when I walk back. "I'm just telling you how I see it."

"Right," Patricia says.

The attendant grins at me. "Your sister?"

"Your mother," Patricia says. She leaves the exact change on top of the pump.

"Okay," the attendant says. He shifts his weight evenly as if to jerk a pair of weights over his head. "Give me your best shot."

Patricia ducks her shoulder when I nudge her toward the car.

"Can you believe this character?" she says.

I walk around to the passenger side. "Let's just go," I say.

She tugs once at the stiff green belt at her waist but then opens her door and gets in.

As we pull away from the station the attendant is still standing with his legs apart as if bracing himself. Patricia gives him the finger.

We drive back through the gates of the post, and the guard doesn't even step out of his hut as we pass. Ft. Polk is an ugly post and my mother can't wait for us to be transferred, even though we've only been here a year.

With her hair blowing back I notice a scar on Patricia's forehead.

"Compliments of my stepfather," she says when I ask her about it. "For mouthing off."

We pass post headquarters, where my father works. He recently ordered the building whitewashed and it appears to glow in the dark.

"Whereas you get along with your old man," Patricia says.

There is an edge to her voice and I don't say anything.

The parade field was mown this afternoon and I can still smell the diesel fumes from the tractors.

"Your family was a trip, all right," she says. "Talk about negative vibes."

I stare at the hole in the dashboard where her radio has been taken out.

"You don't talk much about your parents," I say.

"Parent," she corrects me. "I don't count the warrant officer."

The enlisted housing on the post is run down. My father has tried to get the Corps of Engineers involved but everything moves slower in the South. Even the army.

Patricia's stepfather has complained of having to share a duplex with an enlisted family, but there is a housing shortage. My father tells me that they are actually lucky to get something on the base.

Mrs. Sherman is hard of hearing. And fond of television. The result is that Patricia insists that whenever she is home her mother wear earphones to listen to the TV. Otherwise she blasts it loud enough to hear from the street.

"Teddy and I will be in my room," Patricia shouts at her mother, who smiles back as if she's not quite taken it all in.

"Your father's bowling," she says. "I'm watching Perry."

Patricia nods at me. "Perry Mason. They're bringing back the original cast for a two-hour special."

The house smells of kitty litter, even though I've never seen any cats.

At the end of the hall Patricia grabs a towel out of the closet.

"You can snoop around while I take a quick one," she says. "I can't stand the smell of myself."

I follow her into her room.

"We really are different," she says, rummaging through her dresser. "You can't wait to get home and I can't wait to get out."

The bed is unmade and clothes are strewn about the floor. Two large stereo speakers are suspended from the ceiling with nylon fishing tackle. Her stepfather claims she'll get a better sound.

"Five minutes max," Patricia says, and closes the door after her.

After a while I can hear the shower through the thin walls and I imagine Patricia standing beneath the spray. She doesn't need the martial arts to keep in shape. As soon as she graduates she wants to work in a health club a thousand miles from here.

The shower has been off for a while when she leans back into the room, wearing only a towel.

"Damn," she says. "I wanted to catch you at something."

I'm sitting on the bed, reading the liner notes on one of her country-and-western albums.

"How do you like the mattress?" she says.

I press down on it. "Feels like a diving board."

"Hard's good for the spine." She shakes her head at the sound of the TV. "Christ," and pads back down the carpeted hall to shout at her mother to put her earphones on.

When she was eight Patricia tried to kill her stepfather. But the paper-doll scissors were too blunt and barely pierced his uniform. Recently, she thought of trying it again. "Only, with something sharper."

She comes back and kicks the door shut behind her. "That's all she does with her time. Watch that idiot tube." She bends over to brush her wet hair straight down. When she snaps her head back, her face is flushed. "I smell better than you do."

"Much better."

She sits down next to me on the bed and the towel splits open halfway up her thigh. "So what's the secret of your folks' success? They live together, right?"

It's Ivory soap and it smells wonderful.

"Dad hits the road every chance he gets."

"That's the thing. Give each other some breathing room." There are still pearls of water on her bare shoulders. "You can have your family," she says, and leans back on her elbows.

"Do I have any choice?"

"Well," she says, "you probably feel different. But I'll tell you what. If they can just keep an eye out for you. Till maybe you're five or something, then okay. So you don't drown or electrocute yourself. After that I'd say you're better off on your own."

"Six on?"

She nods without smiling. "What about your sister? She blames your mother, right?"

"My mother. Me. My father."

"That's what I mean. You're just asking for it, you stick around too long."

She studies me critically for a moment as if daring me to glance down at the towel.

I stand up and touch one of the speakers, which sends it spinning.

"It's one of the reasons I'm going to school in the fall," I say.

She raises, then lowers, her leg, her foot still pink from the hot shower. "College," she says. It's the same flat tone she used with the service station attendant. "Tell me something," she says finally, her eyes glaring like a sparring partner's. "You think I'm a little dumb, too, don't you? Like your mother and sister."

I'm shaking my head. "That's not true."

"It's like all of you thought you were so much better than what you were looking at. That was a real trip, let me tell you."

I think suddenly of telling her about the perfume bottle. But the whole thing seems ludicrous now.

"I'll take you home," she says, rotating her foot in small circles. It's one of the warm-up exercises in class. "Why don't you see if the old lady's figured out who did it yet. She's good at that."

In fact, Mrs. Sherman has changed channels. "I didn't like Perry so old," she says, the earphones resting atop her head.

I'm sitting on the vinyl sofa, trying to pay attention. But it's as if a trapdoor has opened under me and now I'm in the living room. Patricia is right, of course. It was exactly as she described it. Cora and my mother were condescending and aloof, and instead of telling them both off in front of her, I only tried to gloss it all over afterward.

On the ride home Patricia doesn't say anything until we turn into the officers' housing.

"The other side of the tracks," she says as if talking to herself.

At the house she leaves the engine idling and only nods when I tell her I'll see her in class.

"To tell you the truth," she says bluntly, "I don't think it's your sport."

Then I watch her back the convertible out onto the street and squeal the tires without waving to me.

It's a warm, clear night and I sit down on the porch and think about everything I said to her after she came back from the shower wearing only a towel. It's too late now to say anything, of course. But what I should have said was that they'd been that way because she'd made them every bit as uncomfortable as they tried to make her. It had been a great, braless entrance. For once someone had given them a dose of their own medicine. So what if she wasn't Grace Kelly. Who made us the royal family?

The following morning my father and I drive to the post hospital, and beside my exhausted mother, watch Cora, sedated and eyes rolling, get wheeled on a gurney into the operating room. After nearly an hour the captain strolls out to the lobby still wearing his green surgical garb to report that everything went pretty much as anticipated. The only surprise being the relative size of the goiter. It had been a good deal larger than he expected. In fact, one of the larger benign tumors he's ever removed. But happily none of it had any effect on the actual width of the cut. In six months the thin incision would fade from sight and not even her family would likely notice it.

But then the good doctor has the wrong family. Nothing, I'm convinced, ever quite escapes the critical net of my sister. And should something miraculously manage to winnow past her, there is always my mother trawling close behind. Only, today I can't hold anything against either of them. Babbling incoherently under the powerful anesthetic, her eyes big as fists, Cora has to be kept from tumbling off the narrow cot in the recovery room. And so each of us takes shifts watching over her. We could all go home for a nap and come back in a few hours when, as the captain assured us, the patient would be more rational. However, as my mother tried to explain between her tears, no one, not even someone who had operated on her (and she'd seized his hand, raising it reverently to her lips as if he were Prince Rainier himself), not even as wonderful a surgeon as he was could ever really know what was going on inside a child like its own family.

IN
the
GRASS

"My brother, the real estate mogul," Cora says. She steps over the freshly painted molding I've set out to dry on newspapers. "No wonder HUD's giving them away."

In the kitchen she shakes her head at all the cabinet doors stacked against the wall.

"Jesus, and look where he keeps the Cheerios. Under the sink with the Clorox."

Cora will finish up at UCLA this summer and so her visit home has to be short. We are living in Baton Rouge now, where my father heads the ROTC program, the largest in the South. Cora is staying on campus with my parents in the Commandant's House, an enormous antebellum home where Zachary Taylor supposedly once slept.

Upstairs, I follow my sister down the narrow, unlighted hall ("This the rite of passage?") to the bedroom.

"A hammock," she says. "And get a load of the victory garden." She kneels over the rows of starter pots by the space heater. "What in God's name are you growing?"

"I thought I'd try some radishes. There's full sun this side."

"Radishes," she says. "Of course. What was I thinking?" But she's dusting her hands off again. "All right, I'll give you this much. You're out of the house. You don't have to listen to those two anymore. But, Christ, Teddy. This the best you could come up with?"

"The closing costs were less than they'd be paying to keep me in the dorm."

"All Mom talks about," my sister says, "is how her college boy's going to blow the formative years. Over here banging away at some white elephant instead of hitting the books."

I ask her how she thinks Mom's getting along now that the nest is more or less empty.

"Fretting, mostly. Over the prodigal son. And having seen what the prodigal's gotten himself into, I can't blame her." Cora smiles, squinting at me. "So where's *la femme,* kiddo? I've *cherchez*'d everywhere."

"You might try the public library," the student worker at the reference desk suggests.

I tell her I already have and when she shrugs her shoulders, I notice how her breasts rise with the gesture. Then she asks me what kind of carpentry project I'm into and I start in about the house.

"Sounds like an obsession," Janice says to me later. It's her lunch hour and we've walked over to the student union.

I mention how after a couple semesters of college I wanted to do something with my hands. How I thought renovating an old house over the summer would be exciting. Then I go into how I've already spent next year's tuition to cover some hidden expenses.

"How'd that go over with the folks?" she says.

"My mother wanted to know what was wrong with getting an education first. She said I had the rest of my life to get excited."

Janice nods sympathetically. "Sounds like a mom to me. All she wants is the best for her boy. Am I right?"

I admit that she is.

"Well," she says, "if it's any consolation, I don't think you're the first guy ever disappointed his mother."

"Probably not."

"There you are," she says brightly. "Got to be true to your school."

* * *

To keep from thinking about the termites, I spend the rest of the afternoon ripping off wallpaper in the den. Beneath the tacked-up cheesecloth are pressed the droppings of countless cockroaches. Each time I tear another strip from the ceiling, the tiny black pellets rain down upon me. The hardwood floor looks like a sea of caviar. Afterward, when I've finished vacuuming, I stand under the shower for nearly twenty minutes lathering my hair until my scalp aches.

"Enough to do Europe for the summer," Cora said before driving over to the mall, "and he blows it on the enchanted cottage."

The following morning I rent a power sander to strip the oak floor of several layers of yellowed varnish. But the coarse bands of sandpaper are difficult to pry onto the belt and cut deep gashes into the wood.

"You need a pro for that sort of work," my sister says on the way over to the med school's library. "You know. Someone with a calling in life."

My hands have developed thick calluses from smoothing the joint compound on the Sheetrock. Wearing only shorts, I tie a handkerchief over my nose to help keep from breathing the grainy particles that cloud the air. And still my nostrils become so clogged that in bed I cough up wads of thick white dust. My hair is continually tinted a soft silver gray.

"Very distinguished," Cora says when she gets back from campus. She stands by the door as I sit atop the stepladder sanding the strip of Sheetrock over the fireplace. "You look like one of the stiffs they dug out of Vesuvius."

But when the air grows as thick as a pool hall's, she waves her hand in front of her face.

"This supposed to be the home you never had? An army brat's idea of permanence? Because considering what you shot the wad on, I find that ironic."

I have dinner with my mother and sister. Even without central air conditioning the Commandant's House is as cool and damp as a cellar. The walls are packed with Spanish moss gathered by slaves a hundred and fifty years ago. Ancient, motor-powered fans turn slowly overhead from the high ceilings.

Cora complains that after L.A. it's like living in a time warp.

"I feel like ordering a hoop dress," she says. "I wouldn't last fifteen minutes here. It'd be like Chinese water torture."

"Oh, I don't know," my mother says. "You're here awhile, you get used to it."

"What about Dad?" Cora says. "He used to it?"

My father is working late. He's in the middle of a recruiting drive.

"Your father's never been able to sit still for very long," my mother says. "It's just his nature."

"Whereas his son can't wait to sink in his roots," Cora says. "No pun intended."

"What's wrong with settling down?" I say. "We've already seen the world."

"You mean *Dad's* seen the world," my sister says, scraping her chair back from the table in the cavernous dining room. "We haven't seen, pardon my French, *merde*."

"That's not true," my mother says. "You've been all across this country."

"Mom," Cora says, "I hate to break this to you, but this country ain't the world."

My sister believes that we missed out on Europe and half a dozen other overseas assignments only because my mother wouldn't fly.

"Well, I guess it's what you do with where you are," I offer.

Cora smiles at my grim-faced mother. "Almost makes you wonder what the little renovator's been up to over there."

"I've always had this physical thing about books," Janice says, raising both arms over her head in the hammock.

My sister has taken in the afternoon matinee at the University Theater. No doubt because I mentioned that a friend ("So *that's* what the little renovator's been up to") might be stopping by.

"I just like being around them," Janice is saying. "Physically."

Last year, she'd quit her part-time job at the branch library downtown because of the way they manhandled their collection. "I couldn't stand it anymore. Everything from cutting holes in the dust jackets to crushing spines in these huge sorting bins. Books have personalities for me. Anyway, it was criminal, so I quit. Of course, it didn't help that my immediate supervisor also happened to be a lech."

I tell her it's one of the things I like best about the renovating. It's the first summer I haven't had a boss.

"It's great," she says, and swings both feet out of the hammock. "I could move right in."

I'm sawing off dead branches from the cedars when Janice rides her bike up onto the front lawn.

"Got the stickers," she says, and disappears into the house.

When I come in for a glass of water, I find her sitting cross-legged on the floor, surrounded by stacks of books which she's carted down from upstairs.

"You're getting a modified Dewey decimal," she says, and licks one of the gummed labels. "You can go right to what you want now. It'll save you all kinds of time."

I watch her affix several more call numbers before she untucks her blouse from her jeans.

"God, it's hot in here," and she fluffs her short sleeves. "Anyway, I wanted to ask you about your sister. Why we haven't crossed paths. I'm just sort of curious."

I look down at my father's pruning shears. "I don't know," I say finally. "I guess unconsciously I try to keep anyone I like from meeting a blood relative."

Janice nods thoughtfully.

"More likely it's because I don't want to have to hear what they think," I say. "Even though I don't especially care what they think anymore."

"Your sister?"

"My sister. My mother. They're like Scylla and Charybdis."

Janice looks at me. "In other words you don't want the hassle of bringing anyone home because they're so critical."

"Right."

"It'd be like putting someone through the gauntlet?"

"Exactly."

She seems to consider this. "That explain this place?"

"Could be."

"Interesting."

"Pathetic's probably closer to it."

"Oh, I don't know," she says. "Nothing wrong with aiming to please."

"It's *who* I aim to please is the problem," I say. "That's what I'm working on."

"That and an old house."

"That and an old house," I say. "Works in progress."

The following morning my mother's legs are bothering her too much to drive down to New Orleans and so she says good-bye to Cora at the house. My father is off at some ROTC convention in Atlanta. As I wedge Cora's suitcase into the trunk of the VW, she looks back up at the enormous house the university offers rent free to the commandant of cadets. In the shade of the columned front porch my mother waves to us from her rocker.

"All that's missing is a couple of mint juleps," my sister says. "And the commandant, of course."

On the ride down to the airport Cora wears her sunglasses and seems not to notice the spectacular scenery of the bayous. When I point out egrets nesting in the cypress like Christmas ornaments, she barely seems to turn her head. We wind up listening to the radio.

At the airport I pull into short-term parking just as a plane thunders overhead. Cora leans forward, craning to see the jet through the cracked windshield of the VW.

"What do you think it is with Mom?" I say. "Why she'll never get on one?"

My sister makes her patented snorting sound. "Because opposites attract and Dad jumps out of them. Next question."

When she gets like this there's no use in trying to make intelligent conversation. I'm her younger brother. End of discussion. Still, it rankles. How often do I get to see her anymore and yet we haven't managed two intelligent words to each other the entire week. I want to blame Janice's presence but, of course, it's nothing new.

"Traveling light," I say, lifting her suitcase from the trunk.

"The only way to go, kiddo. No commitments."

"What about grad school?" I say. "You're committed to that, aren't you?"

She ignores the question as if the answer is obvious.

"So what's your little friend like?" she says. "Out there pulling crab grass together. It was enough to bring tears to my eyes."

Several times she'd seen Janice's bike and driven by without stopping.

I follow her across the parking lot. In the bright sunlight the concrete is like a white lake. Cora wears mirrored sunglasses that I can see my own reflection in.

"Janice?" I say. "I guess you'd have to say she's very honest. Very straightforward. Someone who doesn't care all that much what other people think. It's too bad you didn't get to meet her."

Cora breezes past me through the automatic doors of the terminal. "I'll try to catch her at the pageant. What's her state?" She glances both ways before spotting her airline counter. "So anyway, what's Wonder Woman do for a living?"

Even though we are early, my sister hurries ahead of me, her carry-on bag thumping against her hip.

I'm lugging the suitcase and am half out of breath keeping up with her.

"To tell you the truth," I say, "I don't think it much matters to her *what* she does for a living. Janice has her own agenda."

Cora's sunglasses bob at the end of her nose as she turns to peer over the top of them at me.

"I have this theory about brothers," she says. "Very Margaret Meadish. Want to hear it?"

"Shoot."

"It's sort of tribal, actually." And she stops to glance up at the board to see that her flight is on time. "The whole thing is for them *not* to marry their sister. So they bend over backward to find her opposite."

"You should try to get your mind off the house," Janice says. She sets her book down. "Take a day off and just relax."

I am lying on the mattress watching a cockroach search for an opening between the exposed pine planks of the ceiling. "Your sister thought the house had a lot of possibilities," my mother said to me on the phone the other day. I could just imagine how that translated into Cora's words. "She only had a few reservations about the neighborhood." I asked if Dad was still awake. "His trip took it out of him," she said. "He was up till two last night watching some Japanese movie your sister recommended." I wondered how her legs were doing. "Your mother's just an old war bride," she said. "You're the only one ever worries about me anymore."

After a brief thundershower the sun comes back out and I try working in the yard, but Janice sees that I'm dawdling and suggests a bike ride instead.

"Maybe it'll help snap you out of it," she says.

I toss the hand trowel on top of the clump of unplanted monkey grass.

"Won't that dry up in the sun?" she says.

When I shrug my shoulders, she looks at me curiously.

We take University Avenue down past the faculty housing and onto the dirt path around the lake. As we approach the stretch of cypress knees along the bank, Janice jumps off her bike and lets it career into the deep weeds.

"Come on," she says excitedly, and I watch her run across the path, then cut in toward where the snakes sun themselves. After skidding to a stop I pry the kickstand down and walk back.

It's no more than five yards from the bike route to the water's

edge, but every inch is thick with growth. Some of the weeds reach
to my waist and I have to part them like curtains, when abruptly I
come upon Janice. She is sitting on the damp scrub grass with her
blouse untucked. Just behind her in the water the moccasins are
entwined about the cypress limbs.

"Come on," she says. "Forget about the house." When she lies
back I notice how white, almost translucent, her skin seems in the
sunlight, and as the snakes begin to move ominously on the stumps,
my heart is pumping so fast, it's hard to hear her beside me.

"Think about your books," Janice whispers. "Think about how
they're all alphabetized now."

One of the thicker moccasins slides into the dark water, moving
along the surface, its head up like a tiny periscope.

"How about I think about you?" I say.

She pries her sneakers off, stretching her legs out in the grass. "So
what do you think?"

What I think is that she is nothing like us. She is not
hypercritical. She does not read her horoscope as if it were a medical
prescription. She does not own a Ouija board. She does not know
why Liz left Eddie. She does not subscribe to *Lotto,* the international
journal for lottery lovers. She is a registered voter. She lives on and
cares about the future of this planet. All of which, of course, is
exactly my sister's point. No one would ever mistake her for one of
the family.

"You're so tense," Janice says. "You're tight as a harp."

But just then, right across the lake, I notice that a magnificent
rainbow has arched out of the clouds to touch down on the
Commandant's House, my parents' temporary home, as regal and
permanent as I imagine someday my own place to be.

GOOD HEARTS

When she got bored with graduate school, Cora surprised us all by coming back East and marrying a doctor. What *didn't* surprise me is that he's apparently a lot older than her. How much older, my mother won't venture over the phone. "Anton's Romanian," she says the day I get her letter. "It's hard to say with foreigners." But when she refuses to hazard a guess, I know we aren't talking about any beach boy. "Anton's a very distinguished man," my mother adds. "He went to the Sorbonne. He's a heart specialist." Cora met him last summer when my father got her a job editing training films at the military labs where he is now director. The people there work with NASA dreaming up things like granola bars made from the space crew's own fecal matter. "Nutritional supplements," the scientists call them, but my sister tells me that they taste like what they are.

Two years ago my father was assigned to the army research facility outside Boston. They've only recently bought a house and so I have to ask for directions.

"It's a little off the beaten path," my father says. "Your mother picked it out. If the roof lasts the winter I'll be thrilled."

Of course, what I really want to hear about is my new brother-in-law, only my father's conspicuously avoiding the subject.

"Even the Century 21 gal tried to talk her out of it," he is saying. "Not a real healthy sign."

But these are long-distance rates and I know when my father is stonewalling.

"So," I say at last. "A real doctor in the house. Even if he *is* a little long in the tooth."

I can hear my mother kibitzing at his elbow.

"That's the least of it," he offers finally. "Believe me."

In the morning before leaving I drop off a late makeup paper and my overdue books. I've switched majors again and am auditing a few courses in landscape architecture. I leave a message on Janice's answering service asking if she'll take some notes for me in class today. Actually, it's just an excuse to talk to her when I get back. I decided against inviting her to come up with me. And that's caused some friction. But we've already been through Meet-the-Family once before and I don't see the point of putting us through it again.

With frigid air blowing through the VW's heater vents, I have to pull off the freeway every other Howard Johnson's to thaw my toes. Usually I wait for the men's room to clear before using one of the hand dryers. But sixty miles from my exit my feet are so cold, I don't care who sees me.

It's snowing and I've lost all tactile sense by the time I reach the Route 9 cutoff. The rambling, three-storied Victorian house is on one of the finger lakes near Framingham. I turn down the snowplowed dirt road and the signs of neglect are immediate. Still, the house sits atop high ground and there's a lovely panoramic view of the lake. As soon as the VW's engine clatters off, my mother appears on the wide, screened-in porch.

"Your father's getting his lottery tickets," she says, eyeing the car. "I thought you were going to get rid of that."

I follow my mother into the large foyer. Because of the oil prices they've closed off most of the downstairs. We cross through the chilly dining room to the parlor, where I quickly back up against the crackling fire.

"Your father's been buzz-sawing up a storm," my mother says. She eases down into the wing chair like an old person. "Two weeks ago you couldn't see the house from across the lake. He's cut a path out there like a meteor."

I tug my shoes off, my feet prickling agreeably with the warmth of the fire.

"How're your legs doing?" I ask. She'd winced lifting them up onto the footstool.

"I wish I could saw them off, honey."

But that's as much as I'll get her to say. She'll no more see anyone about them than join the Officers' Wives Auxiliary. My mother has never been interested in anyone's health but her family's.

"So when do Dr. Frankenstein and his bride get here?" I say.

The newlyweds have rented a bungalow across the lake.

"You know your sister," my mother says.

But I'd never go that far.

"Tell me the truth," I say, trying to draw her in. "How much do you know about this guy? I mean, Cora can't have known him that long."

My mother's eyes narrow but we both turn at the sound of my father in the hall, his jump boots thumping on the hardwood floor.

Reunions tend to be awkward in my family. We're not, as Janice likes to say, a particularly kissy-huggy household. My father is wearing his Eisenhower jacket, his earlobes red as a thermometer bulb. And when I reach out to shake his hand he hesitates as if trying to recall the meaning of the custom.

"Heard you got some tickets," I say.

He opens his wallet. "I played your birthday."

But when I look at the numbers I see that he's confused the date with Cora's.

"I'll get the hot water heater going," my mother says, shooting a last warning look at my father. "Your sister and Anton are supposed to be here at eight."

My father moves the screen aside to set another small log in the fire. It's obvious that he's had the clamps put on him.

"So tell me about Dr. Kildare," I say. "What's an M.D. doing in a research lab?"

My father seems to weigh his response for a moment. "Not there anymore."

The hot water pipes rattle overhead.

"He's not?"

My father rotates his head slowly. "Nope."

"There was a problem?"

He closes his eyes, nodding just as slowly. "Yep."

I listen to the shower running upstairs. "You're not allowed to volunteer anything but it's all right to answer yes or no?"

"Yes."

"This problem," I say. "Are we talking mental or physical?"

"Yes."

I look down at my feet. "Mental?"

He nods.

"So," I say, suddenly less enthusiastic about the game. "Cora's catch ain't such a catch."

My father doesn't stop nodding.

It's almost a relief when my mother knocks on the upstairs bathroom wall. The water is ready.

She's set out monogrammed towels and my father's shaving kit. "So, you and your girlfriend . . ." my mother says, adjusting the taps on the huge porcelain tub. "You're still seeing each other?"

"Touch and go," I say. "But I guess a little more touch right now than go."

"Well, maybe now you can concentrate on your books a little more," she admonishes me. "Stop flitting around from one subject to the next. You have a perfectly good mind."

I study my hair in the pitted, beveled mirror. It's starting to thin out at the temples.

"That's what comes from not listening to your mother," she says, peering over my shoulder. "You wouldn't be going through this now."

"What? A receding hairline?"

"You know what I'm talking about."

She sets new underwear out for me. The T-shirt still has the gray cardboard sheet in it.

"What about Anton?" I say. "Still got it all on top?"

"Your brother-in-law's a doctor. He doesn't need any hair."

Later, from the upstairs landing, I see a Yellow Cab pull up in front of the house. The shutters on the living-room window are open and I watch my sister lean over the seat to pay the driver.

Cora strides in ahead of Anton. They're both wearing fur coats.

"You look ten years older," my sister says as soon as she sees me. Her breath is visible in the cold foyer. "Anton." And she turns indifferently to her husband. "My sibling."

"Ah, yes," Anton says, trying to peel his kid glove off. His thick accent is only the second shock about him. The first is his age. He's at least as old as my father. But considerably shorter and more rotund. "You are Cora's younger brother."

"Even if he doesn't look it anymore," my sister says, and leads the rest of us back to the parlor.

"No car?" I say to Anton, who keeps his fur hat on.

He appears stumped by the question and looks to his wife.

"At the shop," Cora says, glaring at both of us.

In the parlor my father only glances over the top of his bifocals, then resumes reading the paper.

Anton straddles the arm of the wing chair. There's the mad-scientist look about him: stray strands of hair twist up from his bushy eyebrows.

"Cora say you want to draw landscape," he says genially. "There is money in this?"

"Not the way I do it."

"Mr. Modesty," Cora says. "As a matter of fact, my brother has very good taste. In art."

The allusion escapes my brother-in-law, of course. My sister refuses to ask me anything about Janice. The one time they met, they did not, to no one's surprise, hit it off.

Anton pulls down a small leather bag from the bookcase.

"It is time for the checkup," he says, and draws a stethoscope from the black satchel. "Everybody, raise the sleeve, please."

My mother suddenly appears at the door. "Good," she says. "Just enough time before dinner."

My brother-in-law has apparently gotten into the habit of checking everyone's blood pressure. He starts with my father, who keeps the paper folded in his lap.

"Everybody in this family has a good heart," my mother says as soon as Anton finishes with her.

I sit down on the couch beside my brother-in-law. His pinstripe suit is rumpled, his silk tie knotted haphazardly. After wrapping the Velcro about my arm, he pumps the rubber ball, concentrating intently. And for the first time I am persuaded that he is, in fact, a doctor.

The vein in my wrist throbs as Anton releases the valve on the armband. He nods silently with each count of pressure.

We all wait for the verdict until my brother-in-law at last looks up.

"Once more," he says too loudly, the stethoscope still in his ears.

My mother wipes her hands on her apron. "It doesn't mean anything," she assures me. "He'll just double-check when it's someone he hasn't done before."

Anton bows his head as if to hear better and I notice his bald spot, as perfect as a yarmulke. He lowers the stethoscope about his neck and hesitates as if still uncertain about his reading.

"Okay," my brother-in-law says without looking up. "Now we go to eat."

My mother is all smiles. "What did I tell you. Everybody in this family has a good heart."

The single radiator in the dining room is turned up as far as it will go, and the door into the kitchen is left propped open for the heat from the stove. Yet by dessert it's cool enough for a sweater.

"So why didn't you bring us some drawings?" Cora says. She's on a diet and picks at the chocolate icing Anton has left on his plate.

"You see one picture, you've seen them all."

My mother shakes her head. "How are businesspeople going to take you seriously if you don't take yourself seriously?"

She's embarrassed for me in front of her accomplished son-in-law. But I doubt that Anton has heard a word of it. He sits beside Cora sketching a Rube Goldberg–like contraption on his paper

napkin. Every once in a while he blurts out something in Romanian
to himself and then erases furiously. I'm sorry Janice can't be here to
meet him. She's a psych major.

With the radiator clacking annoyingly all of us retreat to the
parlor with our coffee cups. Except my father. There's a *National
Geographic* special on, and he wanders upstairs to the television in
the bedroom.

I turn the log over in the grate. "We need some wood."

"Your father will come down later," my mother says. She's been
watching Anton uneasily. He's smoothed something out on the floor
that looks like a blueprint. And then I can see that it's the same
machine he sketched on his napkin, only in more detail.

"Where's the woodpile?" I ask my mother.

Anton lets the drawing curl back up. "I will help," he says.

"Just a small log," my mother concedes.

Once outside, my brother-in-law pulls his pack of Gauloises
greedily from his coat. Cora won't let him smoke in the same room
with her.

"I must speak to you about your habits," Anton says. His breath
whistles in the cold.

But I'd suspected as much. He's kept quiet until my mother
wasn't around.

"Your diet," my brother-in-law says solemnly. "No more red
meat. No more salt. No more like what your momma make tonight.
These are the habits you must break."

"No more pasta," I say. "Hurt me."

Anton inhales deeply. "This can be worse," he muses, and then
crushes the empty cigarette pack as if it were my heart. "You can be
dead."

We come back around the house, each of us cradling a small log
in our arms. Shuffling in front of me in his dark fur coat and hat, my
burly brother-in-law looks like a washed-up circus bear. I don't
understand my sister. Why she would give up graduate school to
marry a man twenty years older than her. A man who barely speaks
her language, in every sense of the word. A man she already holds

in contempt. But then who did I expect? Louis Pasteur? My sister isn't exactly Madame Curie.

It's after one and I'm reading in the parlor when my father comes down in his robe to check on the fire.

"Still a little wound up from the trip," I say.

He lifts the other log up with the pincers.

"Point of information," I say, but he keeps his back to me. "Why'd Anton blanch when I asked about their car?"

It's the least of my questions, but I don't want to scare him off. My father nestles the log onto the grate.

"It's a touchy subject," he says. "Your brother-in-law's not supposed to drive."

I know that with all the medication Cora has to take no insurance company would touch her, but no one has said anything about Anton. "Why not?"

My father holds his hands out to the fire and smiles over his shoulder at me. "Because the judge said he couldn't."

Just last month Anton had run a red light and slid into a snowbank.

"And they suspend your license for that?" I say.

My father yawns, closing his eyes and tilting his head back. "Not if you're wearing your clothes. That's where your brother-in-law went wrong."

By the time a squad car arrived on the scene, Anton had stuffed every stitch on his back into the glove compartment.

"Mercedes have a larger-than-average glove compartment," my father adds.

After meeting my parents Janice described my father as "laconic." He was the only one she managed to get along with.

"So what are we talking about here?" I say. "Just the tip of the snowbank or what?"

My father smiles crookedly. "Funny you should mention snowbanks. He emptied your sister's jewelry box into one just the other day."

I ask if Cora has him going to anyone, a psychiatrist.

"Your sister," my father says. "She and your mother make a great pair: See No Evil and Hear No Evil."

"So why don't you say something to him?"

He rubs his palm across his chapped lips. "We talking about the same guy? Look, you call some doctor's secretary, she tells you the patient has to come in on his own volition."

"Did you tell them Anton's an M.D.?"

"I told the first one that. She practically hung up on me. Head doctors don't like to see heart doctors with head problems. Something to do with insurance and lawsuits."

"What kind of sense does that make?"

My father shrugs his shoulders wearily. "It's been my experience."

Thursday afternoon Cora calls to ask if someone will pick up Anton. He's missed the last commuter bus in from Natick. Apparently he has started doing some kind of consulting work in Boston now that he's no longer at the labs. My father has just gotten home from work and puts his coat back on slowly.

"Take your son," my mother says, and holds the car keys out. "Let him pick some numbers."

The station wagon is still warm, and my father adjusts the rearview mirror, turning his jaw as if to shave. "They don't know the first thing about this character," he says.

The sharpness of his tone surprises me. But then, he's had a long day at the office.

"They know he's a doctor," I say. "I guess that's all they need to know."

We wait at a light, the engine chugging in the cold.

"He gives physicals for some insurance companies in the city," my father says. "I doubt he can even practice in this country."

I've decided to head back early. Midterms are coming up and I'm on probation.

In town, gray meter heads poke up through the plowed snow.

"Well, what do you know," my father says, cutting sharply into an empty lot.

At first, I imagine one of the chains has fallen off. But when we come to a complete stop, my father turns off the engine.

"Show time," he says, and sets the hand brake.

The hood ornament of the station wagon is pointed directly at a bus stop across the street. There's a single empty bench with a see-through weather shield.

"By the hydrant," my father says, lifting his chin slightly.

I hunch forward. "What is it?" It looks like a tarpaulin.

"Your brother-in-law," my father says. "The doctor."

I jerk the door handle down but my father reaches across me.

"Relax," he says calmly. "He's all right."

"He's all right! It's ten degrees out there."

My father lets go of my arm. "What do you think, this is something new?"

But he can see that I'm upset.

"Okay, okay," he says, unlocking the door. "Take it easy."

I trot ahead of him across the street. It's Anton, all right. Flat out on his back, his coat open and his shirt unbuttoned to the waist. But he doesn't seem in any physical pain.

"Anton," I say, and kneel beside him. "Can you get up?"

His eyes are open, his barrel chest pink from the cold.

"Tell him his mother-in-law's got dinner on," my father says from the bench.

"Why don't you sit up," I try coaxing him. "You must be freezing."

But he only gazes serenely past me. It's impossible to be angry with him. It's my mother and Cora I blame.

My father comes back from the station wagon. "Let's try this," he says, holding his fist out. "It's worked before."

There are half a dozen paper clips in his palm and he sets one down on Anton's bare chest.

"Found them in the car," my father says when Anton flinches. "I thought they might be from the Reduction Machine."

I look at my father.

"Something your brother-in-law's been working on," he says. "For heart stress. Those were the blueprints in the parlor."

For the first time Anton appears to be paying attention.

"Trouble is," my father says, "there's no copyright on the damn thing."

Anton pushes up onto his elbows, the paper clips sliding off his chest. "'S.P.,'" he whispers.

I stare blankly at my father.

"Solar power," he explains. "Your brother-in-law's machine relies on the sun. That's what he's been doing out here, absorbing the rays." My father pretends to lower his voice so that Anton can't overhear. "I worry about somebody stealing the idea. Somebody from the labs, for instance."

Then he steers me over to the curb out of Anton's earshot. A squad car turns up the street and we both stiffen. But it passes.

"If I thought there was any chance he might hurt your sister," my father says, "it'd be different. But he's harmless. He clicks in and out every once in a while."

Anton suddenly scrambles to his feet, hops over the fire hydrant, and looks both ways before crossing to the parking lot.

"Let's wait till he's settled in the car," my father says. "You don't want to set him off again."

In town we stop at the drugstore for lottery tickets.

"Let me pick up a few things for dinner," my father says, glancing up at me in the rearview mirror. He wants me to stay with Anton. My brother-in-law sits rigidly in the front seat, twisting a paper clip around his wedding finger.

To break the ice I offer that he might try the Reduction Machine on me. With my blood pressure up so high I seem the perfect candidate for a test run. But when I ask Anton what he thinks of the idea, he only leans one elbow on the dashboard and starts writing an equation across the fogged-up windshield.

"Good advice," I say, and sit back in the seat.

My father returns from the deli with a loaf of pumpernickel, some hard rolls, and a cheesecake.

"I talked to your mother," he says, and hesitates a moment before flicking the defroster on to clear the windshield. "We're supposed to pick Cora up for dinner."

We take a different route back around the lakes. As we pass under an old stone overpass, I ask when Anton is likely to snap out of it. My father smiles wryly in the mirror.

"Soon as he sees your sister."

When we pull up in front of the bungalow, I notice the Mercedes parked in the driveway. The entire grill is mashed in. The car had to have been towed. When my father beeps the horn twice, Anton turns about in the front seat.

"So you have come along for the ride," my brother-in-law says, grinning happily.

I nod. "How you doing?"

Cora inches up the walkway cautiously, her coat pulled back so she can see her feet. "I hate the snow," she is saying. "I hate, hate, hate it." Anton meets her halfway and she seizes his arm. "What'd you sit on?" she says. "Your coat's all wet."

Anton brushes his backside. "Maybe it happens on the bench."

My sister raises an eyebrow at him but doesn't pursue it. When she slides into the backseat next to me, I decide not to ask her anything about the car. And neither does my father.

At the house my mother comes to the door, her face flushed from standing in front of the stove all afternoon. I can tell that her legs are sore. She has that look.

"How'd you get so wet?" she says, and carries Anton's coat into the downstairs bathroom. "It's sopping."

But Anton is as puzzled as my mother.

At dinner Cora talks about how they plan to move into the city soon. Some new apartments are going up near the river.

"Most of them are already presold," she says. "Especially the ones with any kind of view of the water."

Anton's brow furrows. "This place," he interrupts. "Where is this place you are talking about?"

My sister wets her napkin to dab affectionately at his spaghetti-splattered chin. "You remember, honey. I showed you the ad in the *Globe* Sunday."

Anton's bushy eyebrows twitch anxiously.

"What you buy is essentially just the frame," Cora continues, undeterred by her husband's memory lapse. "You bring in your own floor plan. Which is the only way to do it, as far as I'm concerned."

It's after midnight when I drive them back in the station wagon. We all sit in the front seat listening to the tire chains crunch on the packed snow.

I might not see them again and so I come in for a drink. The furnished bungalow is musty smelling and cramped.

"I'm a city girl," Cora says, flopping down on the mildewed sofa. "It's all right for Mom and Dad. But, I mean, we're talking major cultural blight out here."

Anton wheels in a tea caddy on which he's set out cheese and crackers.

"So Mom tells me you're thinking about landscape architecture?" Cora says, making a strained effort to be sociable.

There's no point in asking about her own studies. Why, suddenly, she's given up on her graduate program. Flightiness is obviously a family gene.

"For the time being anyway," I say.

Anton slumps in the La-Z-Boy recliner. He keeps his coat on, unbuttoned, one hand tucked under his arm. I'm too tired to try to include him in the conversation. We both simply listen to Cora and her ambitious interior designs ("The minute I laid eyes on this picture of Merle Oberon in her living room, I said to myself, 'Now, *that's* what I want it to look like'").

When, at last, I mention having to hit the hay, my sister offers no objection and we both push up from the flimsy couch at the same time, nearly tipping it backward.

"Well," Cora says, "guess I'll see you when I see you."

Anton escorts me to the door. When I turn around, my sister is already down the hall.

"Now we may talk," my brother-in-law whispers, squinting ferociously at me. He clamps my forearm like a drowning man. There are other drawings he wants me to see. But because Cora makes him keep them outside, his mildewed blueprints have become "greenprints."

In the cluttered garage Anton flicks on a light bulb to unlock a metal filing cabinet. The printed tabs are all in Romanian and he lifts out several water-spotted manila envelopes.

Then, reaching up, he unhooks an aluminum chaise lounge from the pegboard. "For you," he says, and retrieves a second lounge chair for himself.

My father warned me about letting my brother-in-law pull me off to the side. It didn't take much to uncork the genie from his bottle.

Anton bumps open the door, rattling the awkward chair after him. "Here it is not safe," he says. "Come."

I watch him poke his pointed Italian leather shoe into the crusted snow as if testing his bath. Satisfied that it isn't too deep, he high-steps it halfway down the backyard before I can stop him.

"Anton! For cryin' out loud."

Like a raccoon caught in a car's headlights my brother-in-law gazes back up at me. "This way," he says, his voice husky in the cold.

I pull the lawn chair after me, my pulse throbbing in my throat. It doesn't surprise me that my sister doesn't hear us. Her pills knock her out two minutes after she takes them.

"Wait!" I shout when Anton tries to unfold the rusted chaise lounge. "Just hold it there."

Unable finally to pry it open, he hurls the chair onto the ice, where it skitters twenty feet from shore. But when he steps out onto the ice himself, my heart freezes. I've not seen any kids skating since I got here.

"Christ, Anton!"

He ignores me, inching each foot forward like a tightrope walker. I've no idea how deep the water is. Or how abruptly the shelf falls off.

"This is crazy," I call out to him.

He manages to open the chaise lounge and now eases himself onto it. I stand on the bank trying to coax him back in.

"You'll sink like a rock," I shout, hands cupped into a megaphone. "They won't chip you out till the spring."

He angles the chair so that his back is to me.

"They'll send someone over from the labs," I yell. "He'll get the frozen blueprints and forget about you."

Anton only hikes his thumb up at the moon. It's full and he has his shirt open again, basking in the chaise lounge as if on the deck of an ocean liner.

I haul the garden hose back down from the garage, lassoing the nozzle end out to him.

"Catch hold," I plead, but instead he wriggles up from the folding chair and wraps the hose once about his thick waist. It's a brief tug of war. Even with both heels dug in the snow I'm no match for him. Tumbling out onto the ice, I try to keep my legs from scissoring when Anton snaps his end and I go down heavily.

Some time later when I open my eyes, the hose is tangled about my ankles and I wait for the ice to crack like a fault.

"This lake is not so deep." It's Anton. He's leaning over me, his large head blocking out the moon. "Maybe ten feet here is all. This is nothing."

My ears are thumping and I touch the knot at the back of my head. My left shoe, I notice, is off, the sock stuffed inside. And I understand that I've been unconscious.

"You are sleepy for a little while," my brother-in-law is saying. He runs a car key up my bare foot and nods when my toes curl over. "You see, it is only a bump. There is no problem."

I'm sitting in the chaise lounge in the middle of the lake, the bungalow lost in the distance. Beside me, in the other folding chair, Anton explains how all of this is "made-man," a vast project of the WPA during the thirties. The lakes are artificial, not really real. I believe him but am careful not to shift my weight in the chair. We are, I estimate, roughly the length of a football field from land.

My brother-in-law's fur coat covers my legs. He studies his blueprints, his hair still damp from dragging me across the ice. I neglect to ask how this was managed but suspect that the garden hose, coiled nearby, must have figured into the enterprise. My heel marks recede like train tracks into the dark.

Although the trees obscure my parents' house, I can see vaguely

where the pier juts into the water. It's a toss-up as to whose side of
the lake we're closer to. But when I think of where I am, I
experience a sputtering sensation in my chest, like a propeller
backfiring. My brother-in-law, meanwhile, speaks sotto voce of the
security measures he's had to take to protect his invention. Even
here, he whispers, he must be careful which way the wind is
blowing.

In fact, the chill air is breathless. And yet every imagined sound,
no matter how harmless, causes my heart to stutter-step. Closing
my eyes, I think again about last night. I'd stretched the upstairs
phone into my bedroom to call Janice. I wanted to ask her if there
was any assignment. But then someone whose voice I didn't
recognize answered after the first ring. "Janice?" he asked pleasantly.
"Sure, Janice is here. Hold on a second." While I waited I could hear
faint laughter above the stereo. Then Janice came on. "So what's
up?" she asked finally. But I hadn't planned on this (I'd forgotten
her mentioning she was going to have some people over) and could
think of only Anton's report on my high blood pressure. "Well,
there you are," she said coolly. "Must run in the family, honey.
Everything else seems to." I glanced at my watch, trying to recall in
my confusion if they were an hour later or an hour earlier. "I guess
I better let you go," I offered at last, the receiver warm against my
ear. Janice held the phone away a moment to hush her playful
friend. She came back, her voice tinged with bitterness. "That's
probably not a bad idea, Teddy."

Although it would be foolish to admit it to Anton, I can't deny
the eerie beauty of our perspective. It's as if our lawn chairs have
descended on the vast, pocked crater of another planet. Too cold for
life, everything is tinted blue by a single, orbiting moon. Peering
over the arm of the chaise lounge, I imagine sighting down one leg
of a space probe's landing pod. And try to envision what it would be
like to discover a new world. But somebody over at the labs said in
the paper the other day that if we're ever going to make it to another
galaxy, someone is going to have to have his heart freeze-dried. Or
at least slowed down to where it's more or less in suspended
animation like a goldfish frozen in a pond. It's hard to fathom how

it would feel to have your heart gradually thaw back into life. Still, for all the scientists know, you could wake up without a shred of memory of even your own family, so that from that moment on everything and everyone would be absolutely new.

THE KING
and QUEEN
of REX

Out of the blue Cora phones me from a suite in the Maison La Mont. It's a bad sign. The expensive hotel is the only five-star establishment in New Orleans and I know that she can't afford it. Still, after a year without a word, I'm eager to see her. There is no explanation for the long hiatus other than that my sister is my sister.

And so I don't ask about Anton. Not even *he* could drive her this far South. Only my mother's illness could do that.

As soon as I hang up, I call Janice at the day-care center. After selling the HUD house for a loss, we moved down closer to the city. Then the economy went sour and neither of us has had much luck finding work. Janice tried a couple of different bookstores in the Quarter but recently has been filling in for someone on maternity leave over at the Little Folks Day Care Center.

"So how's Cora sound?" she asks. "Still crazy after all these years?"

That's exactly how she sounded and it depresses me to admit it.

"You think it's safe to go alone, then?" Janice says. She is only half joking. My father has been relaying to us some of Anton's most recent antics.

"I got the impression she wants to keep him under wraps," I say.

Janice laughs, already a little beat from her morning with a classful of three-year-olds. "Sort of like you'll do with me, right?"

"That's not true," I say, even though it is. "You can come if you want. We could take in a parade after."

It's Mardi Gras week and the coldest on record.

"No," she says, yawning into the receiver. "You go ahead. Talk to your sister. Say hi to the doctor for me if he's around."

"You could drop by after work," I say, knowing that she won't. "We can compare notes afterward."

But one of her colleagues needs to use the phone.

"Teddy, I've got to get back to the kids. I'll see you when I see you."

"I'm not staying out late with them," I say. "I'll probably get back before you do."

"Whatever."

"You're sure you don't want to come?"

She is silent for a moment. "Honey, when you don't mean it, don't say it," and she hangs up.

The VW sits in the driveway, its back tires flat. We can't afford the premiums. I hail a cab and the driver gives me the once-over in the rearview mirror.

"Took the king of Bacchus up there the other day," he says. "Jesus, what's his name? Does all the telethons. You can't turn on the tube and not see him."

But Janice hates TV.

"They get 'em all," he assures me. "Everybody who's anybody."

When we pull into the hotel's sweeping horseshoe drive, a porter is at my door before the taxi even rolls to a stop.

I tip the cabbie almost as much as the fare but he only smiles crookedly. He knows a fish out of water when he sees one.

Still, this is the Maison La Mont. And neither the concierge nor the bellman can be friendlier, trained as they are to offer the benefit of the doubt.

At the desk the clerk rings up Cora's room, and I wait in the warm lobby, watching as one Mercedes after the next glides under the portico to receive the same imperial reception. When, at last, the burnished doors to the elevator sweep open, and my sister, wrapped in her full-length fur coat (an early extravagance from Anton, the suitor) steps out, my knees very nearly buckle.

"I know," she admits. "I've put on a few pounds."

But this doesn't tell half the story. My sister is twice the size I remember her. Even her eyes are slits, pushed shut by her Eskimo-fat cheeks.

"Not a word about the hair," she cautions me. "I'm leaving it. I'm not going to live a lie."

I want to say that it's as good a place as any for us to start but I'm speechless. I would not have recognized my own sister on the street. It's not enough to say that she's let herself go. She has become unmoored.

"Let's take a little constitutional," she says. "Work up an appetite. The hotel puts out a fabulous buffet."

An ancient doorman rises from his bench and like royalty my insouciant sister passes her subject without a nod.

Outside, she turns up her collar as if the wind were a personal affront. There has never been a Mardi Gras with temperatures below zero. Still, the crowds are here. Just fewer exhibitionists among them.

To break the ice Cora remarks on the unseasonable cold. It monopolizes the news. The city has opened its gymnasiums to the homeless. Derelicts hover about every warm grate. We step around them even this far from the Warehouse District.

"The weather?" I say contemptuously, as if that is the best she can come up with after our own long chill.

My sister stops before a particularly pathetic soul who teeters on his knees beside a steaming grate. He is swathed, mummy-like, in soiled rags. The unwrapped big toe of one foot is black from either dirt or gangrene or both. It is doubtful he knows the difference anymore. Hunched over, he gazes into the depths of the sewer as if to coax some sturgeon from an ice hole.

Cora stuffs several bills into his empty pork-and-beans can.

"God bless you," the man rasps, his head rotating up at us like a mechanical toy's.

My sister smiles beneficently. She is Mother Teresa and I don't know whether to cry or to wring her neck. I don't give a damn about the weather. I want to know what in hell has been going on with her. But, of course, I don't ask. Around my sister I have always been the sorcerer's apprentice. And I am reminded that nothing is revealed except by indirection. I must keep my ears pricked to what *isn't* said.

"Your brother-in-law's at some symposium," she volunteers.

"In New Orleans?"

She winks at me. "What'd you think? I came unescorted?"

But this is the problem with my sister. I never know when she is lying merely to have the last word.

Cora stops before the window of an exclusive art gallery near the waterfront. A converted loft, it is the kind of establishment to sniff its nose at anyone who can't afford the works on display. In other words, no place for the impoverished like me.

"Let's browse," my sister says, and rings the bell above the brass mail slot.

We are ushered in by a slight man whose plucked eyebrows seem permanently arched. "Madame? Monsieur?"

But when he reaches for my sister's coat, Cora hesitates as if to consider whether the showroom is worth her time. Her glance takes in the magnificently varnished floors and high-tech spiral staircase. She nods finally an appraiser's approval, surrendering her coat with a remarkably nimble twirl.

I have to stand back to take her in. Yet there is no getting around it (in every sense of the word), she dresses elegantly even for her size.

"Cappuccino?" the gallery owner asks, cupping one hand beneath his pointed chin.

"*Deux, s'il vous plaît.*"

I am fairly certain that exhausts my sister's French. But at this point if she started speaking in tongues I wouldn't be surprised.

Our friend's black leather pants swish irritatingly as he retreats.

"So, how's Anton doing?" I ask, tired suddenly of all the pretenses. "We going to get together this visit?"

Cora has stepped over to the first of a series of gouaches in which muscular blacks cut cane in a brake.

"He's supposed to meet one of his cousins at this conference. A lawyer or something from Prague. Anton never tells me much about his family."

"Then you two must have a lot to talk about."

My sister offers me one of her patented smirks. It's as close as she'll come to a compliment.

The owner rattles a tea caddy back across the hardwood floor.

After a quick tour of the gallery Cora and I, empty porcelain cups in hand, stand before a bronze, steroid-muscled nude in the center of the room.

"Probably out of my price range," I say.

My sister glances at me as if at some lint on the sleeve of her fur. "What isn't?"

My mother has told her that I've dropped out of school for the time being. No doubt they both blame Janice. And I run my ravaged tongue across the back of my teeth, silently counting to ten.

Afterward, at the beveled glass door, the gallery owner shakes hands with me like a man who knew all along he was wasting a cup of cappuccino.

Outside, the first breath of cold air is like acid in my nostrils.

Cora is already reaching into her coat for another wad of bills. Ahead of us half a dozen derelicts, like war wounded, lie propped up against a marble office building.

Back at the hotel we cross the deserted dining room to a corner table.

"The buffet today," Cora says to the waiter without bothering to take the menu. "The guava is fresh?"

The man assures us that it has just fallen off the tree.

"*Deux* buffet, then," my sister says, and he backs away like something out of a Swiss cuckoo clock.

I follow Cora to the magnificent array of fruits and vegetables set out on an elaborately carved oak table.

"*Deux* buffet," I say. "Is he still painting?"

My sister ignores me, intent as she is in stacking her chilled plate with guava that, as a matter of fact, *does* look wonderfully fresh.

At the table she snaps her starched napkin at her side like a matador, her plate a shameless cornucopia.

Behind us the constant rush of a waterfall is like Muzak. It is there, of course, to fill in for any gaps in the conversation. But for my sister and me that would require something on the order of Victoria Falls. My mother is seriously ill and absolutely nothing is permitted to be said on the subject. So profound would the breach in family etiquette be. "People deal with things like this differently," Janice has said of my mother's deteriorating condition. "Your sister's always been a dreamer. So she's going to dream it away. Why should that surprise you?"

"I'm curious," Cora says, and just from the tone of the question I know what is coming. She wonders if I have any plans beyond my current dead-end ones.

When I push the *crème brulée* aside, the waiter sweeps down upon it. The La Chute Room has been empty for hours and he is eager for a respite.

"Everything is satisfactory?" he asks my sister.

She gazes at him icily, having sniffed the faint scent of petulance in his voice. "For the moment."

The waiter forces his best five-star smile. "Certainly."

I can't take my eyes off my sister. We can't be related. Our spines are made of entirely different DNA.

"None," I say as soon as the waiter has backed off. "Nothing but dead ends on the horizon."

"Then the family's to abandon all hope?" she says.

"Now *I'm* curious," I say. "Which family we talking about?"

Cora pats the corner of her mouth with her cloth napkin. "You only get one per life, kiddo."

I suddenly want to seize the tablecloth and rip it out from under all the crystal and china and tear off my tie and leap into the goddamn waterfall screaming what a lie it all is. We aren't rich. Never have been, never will be. This is a hand-to-mouth guy sitting here. And that one there, my big, and I mean *really* big sister, can afford it even less.

"Tell me something," I say at last. "That family include Mom?"

But my sister's withering gaze fixes instead upon our hapless waiter.

She calls him over. "We'll be having coffee. And some of your pastries. Whatever's out." She turns back to me. "Speaking of Mom. She's right, you know. That's always been your problem. You don't take yourself seriously enough. You never have."

I dip the end of my napkin in the ice water, pressing it to my forehead. My face is on fire.

"Look," I say. "You want to go on believing we're the Chosen Family, terrific. Go ahead. I just think we're all getting a little long in the tooth for that charade." I stop and look up at the chandelier, trying to calm down. I'm afraid I'll say something about my brother-in-law. How I know all about the bankruptcy and his frequent-flyer trips to Bellevue.

It seems to be the day for tea caddies. The waiter draws one up to our table laden with pastries.

"That's fine," Cora says when he lingers. "You can leave it." She reaches for one of the eclairs and passes it under her nose as if it were a fine cigar. "It's the reason I think your friend never clicked with Mom."

I'd forgotten this favorite tack of hers: using my absent mother as mouthpiece.

"I take it we're talking about Janice here?"

There is, I suspect, a clinical term for it. Perhaps Yahwehism. But over the years my sister has never spoken a single one of my girlfriends' names.

"Mom just thought you needed someone with a little more ambition in her bones. Someone to spur you on."

That was the Christmas I surprised everyone by bringing Janice over to the house. Cora was home for the holiday break and we all drove down to Gramercy to see the bonfires on the levee. It's an old tradition, the bonfires. No one seems to know exactly what they commemorate. But every season great log pyramids are doused with fuel and ignited along the Mississippi as far down as New Orleans.

"Your sister's critical of everybody but herself," Janice remarked after an hour of strained conversation in the station wagon. We were strolling alone along the levee, the fires like oil rigs in the distance.

"Whereas you think I'm just the opposite. Easy on the world but hard on us."

Farther up the levee my father was trying to time his camera to catch the embers as they gushed from one of the crumbling logs. Cora and my mother, bored with the festival, had crossed the street to the firehouse. Folding tables were set up and several marshals busily ladled out homemade gumbo.

"My moral compass," I said. Janice's skin seemed to glow from the light of the fires.

"It's why they don't have any friends," she said. "You know it's true. Who wants to put up with that kind of scrutiny? Heck if I'm sticking around." She did a Jackie Gleason–like imitation, fingers pointing from her forehead. "I mean, feets don't fail me now."

Afterward, we'd both given up any hope of either my mother or sister ever warming to her. And that night, in bed back at Janice's apartment, we tried to make light of the terrible tension all day.

"I forget," Janice said, the electric blanket clicking as it heated up. "Which one's Scylla and which one's Charybdis?"

I turned onto my side. "Didn't Scylla have all the teeth and bark like a dog?"

She laughed.

"I guess that would be my sister," I said.

But then, everything was funnier in the dark.

Cora raises the éclair as if to receive communion, her eyes half closed.

"No ambition," I repeat dumbly.

She finishes chewing and nods. "It's as if you don't aspire."

"Mom's sentiments?"

"She just wonders what you're waiting for."

I look over at our waiter by the maître d's podium. "Probably the same thing he's waiting for: the check." I wind my watch. I have a desperate urge to catch Janice before she leaves work. "I have to get back."

My sister considers her eyes in her compact, then gazes across at me with contempt. "To what?"

I'm tempted to wipe the smirk off her face with one of the cherry jubilees. Instead, I take out my wallet.

"Let me pay for this."

My sister's expression doesn't change. "With what?"

I want to lash out at her. Tell her that at least I live in the real world. The one where mothers die and screwball surgeons with the shakes aren't allowed to practice. In other words, the world she's been trying to imagine away.

"They don't take cash," she says as our waiter whisks over to assist with her chair. "It goes on the room."

I wait in the lobby as Cora jots down something on hotel stationery and leaves it at the desk for the manager.

"A little slap on the wrist for our friend," she says.

Which, of course, is exactly what she'd like to give me, only across the face. Anything to snap her brother out of his lethargy.

"Come up for a minute," she says. "I want to show you something."

Janice is off at five but I can catch the bus on Decatur and be over there in twenty minutes. There is no reason for the rush, of course. I will see her at home. But I can't stop thinking about our conversation. It's as if I abandoned her for my sister.

On the seventh floor Cora slides her room card into the lock, the tumblers clicking until the door opens like a bank vault.

"You're in a hurry," she says, throwing open one of the expansive closets. The racks are empty except for a spectacularly sequined cape and matching mask. She grins as if she's hand-stitched them both herself.

I'm looking around, trying to find some sign of my brother-in-law's presence. But everything has been made up.

Cora backs me out into the hall. "Well," she says coldly, "it's been real."

Only, now I don't want to let her go. I worry that it will be another year of silence. And that next time, instead of a suite, she'll be in a holding cell, or worse, a padded one.

"How about I drop by for a drink a little later?" I say.

It's more of a sigh than a yes as she nods sadly at her unambitious brother.

Janice sits slumped over on the bench across from the day care when I step off the bus. Like my father, she is one of those rare people capable of nodding off in the most public of places.

I sit down beside her and she even wakes like my father: head back, eyes flickering open.

"What?" She leans past me, shivering and still a little dazed. "Where's your sister?"

"Orbiting Pluto."

I put my arm around her. She's wearing the coat she found at a neighbor's garage sale. And I suddenly feel sorry for myself. Some provider.

"So what happened?" she says, tucking her hands between her knees. "What're you doing here?"

At the end of the block I can see the bus, diesel fumes billowing, turn onto Esplanade and head up our way.

"Cora's like strychnine," I say. "You have to take her in small doses."

Janice fishes out her bus pass. I've stopped raising the question of marriage. She says if the time is ever right again, we'll know it. But her coolness on the subject is still unnerving.

The empty bus rattles down upon us and I'm tempted to stand up my sister.

"Remind me to tell you what one of the kids said today," Janice says, raising her voice.

"Tell me now."

The bus squeals to a stop directly before her.

"He asked me if I'd be his mommy." She steps back as the bus rocks from its heavy idling and the door hisses open. "He thought it'd be nice to have one at home and one at school."

"Bright kid."

She bounds up the steps, holding out her pass for the driver. Then with one arm hooked around the pole, she hunches over to look back at me. "Guess who he reminded me of?" she shouts.

But the driver doesn't wait for my answer.

It's dark by the time I get back to the hotel. When Cora doesn't answer her phone I wait for over an hour in the lobby. This, of course, is her way of getting back at me, having surmised the reason I had to rush off. "If there's one thing I like about your sister," Janice will say, "it's that she honestly doesn't believe anyone's good enough for her brother. At least not in this world."

I leave a note at the desk and walk back down Esplanade. There's an early parade on Poydras and I cross over to Canal Street to watch it unwind toward the Quarter.

But it's too cold to be outdoors and so I find a small bar on Julia Street where the Mardi Gras special is two hurricanes for the price of one. I don't believe for a minute that Anton is around anymore. But then I never got the impression that my brother-in-law was more than a blip on Cora's emotional cardiogram. It's not that my sister is heartless. Only that she marches to a different beat. She is running away from her marriage for the same reason she is running away from her mother's illness. It is not her idea of a double feature.

Happy Hour is over and I lower both feet from the stool. Already I regret the second hurricane. It is a potent concoction. I decide against giving Janice a call. She will want to come pick me up.

Outside, it takes me longer than usual to button up my coat. The uneven brick streets of the Quarter are murder on drunks and so I keep my head down to watch my step. All the way up the boulevard men in rags warm themselves beside smoldering trash barrels. Occasionally something soaked in gasoline will explode, sending whoever is standing too close to the barrel reeling back from the flames.

At the hotel, for some reason, my heart begins to race when I ask the concierge to ring my sister's room again. It is as if I already know what he is about to tell me.

"Madame has checked out."

I glance down at the ledger as if to correct his mistake. But I have to step back to keep my balance. When I look up again, the concierge is studying me critically.

"When you say she's gone," I manage finally, bracing my hip against the high counter, "do you mean she's square with you people?"

The man tilts his head slightly and I'm thinking how unpleasant the French can be.

"I mean," I say, "did she pay her goddamn bill?"

An elderly couple have come up behind me. And I know that I am causing a delay and even creating a little scene and that in a moment the doorman will be over here.

"Fine," I say, both hands up. "Terrific. No problem."

Only, now the doorman *is* moving toward me. Then someone in a uniform asks if I might keep my voice down.

"Hey, I'm out of here," I tell him.

But just to be certain, two bouncers dressed as bellhops seize me by the elbows and without so much as a word we move discreetly toward a door. It isn't a door I've noticed before. And on the other side, as it turns out, is an alley.

Neither of my young escorts bears me the least ill will. Indeed, they both wish me a hearty *"Bonne chance."*

Nevertheless, I am standing in the cold. Apparently right outside the hotel's kitchen. There is the scent of nouvelle cuisine in the air.

It's a clear night and after a while I look up to find the North Star. However, it's the distant sound of a parade that gives me my bearings.

At an all-night liquor store off St. Peter's I buy a jumbo bottle of Dixie. It's the one place in America where the cops won't hassle you about an open container.

The floats are backed up half a mile on Canal. Bored Shriners sit waiting on their midget funny cars, sick from inhaling their own exhaust. Behind them the high school band from DeRidder perches on their helmets in the street. The cheerleaders, freezing in mesh stockings and skimpy skirts, pass the time flirting with gangs of males who shout obscene suggestions to them. They are separated by a barricade of brawny chaperones.

I am leaning against the window of a pawnshop when a thunderclap of cheering makes me look up. A mammoth papier-mâché float shimmies through a sea of waving arms, bumping down Canal like some Gargantua in a low-budget film. The crowd is showered with gold doubloons. Great gobs of plastic necklaces are slung overhead as I'm swept forward, helpless against the frightening undertow of bodies. Suddenly on my knees at the curb, I gaze up to catch in a kind of tunnel vision the most fabulous krewe of all, the burly king and queen of Rex, waving stiffly to their supplicants: a masked brother-in-law and sister bright as twin stars in their sequined robes.

MY FATHER'S GEISHA

The sudden revelation of my father's adultery has been unsettling to my sister and me. That the woman is Oriental and apparently has known my father for years hasn't helped.

"The man is kicking sixty," Cora argues long distance. "Who does he think he's kidding?"

Darlene, her roommate, picks up the extension downstairs. "Hi, Teddy."

"For instance, that she's just a houseguest," my sister is saying. "That's been my personal favorite. I mean, let's get with the program."

My father has retired and is still living in the old house on the lake. Up until last month, we thought, alone.

"The last time he was overseas," Cora says, "Mom joked about how he'd probably wind up running off with some Chink in a pedicab. Well, she wasn't so far off."

My mother passed away last year. She had let her health go for so long that when she came down with a simple cold it quickly escalated into pneumonia. Two weeks later she lapsed into a diabetic coma. But now my sister is convinced that the real cause was a broken heart—my mother having found out about my father's geisha.

Just for the sake of argument I offer that maybe the woman *is* his houseguest. From both receivers there comes an audible sucking in of breath.

"Are you serious?" Darlene says.

It's a moment before Cora seems to gather herself. "Oh, he's serious, all right. Seriously out of it, per usual."

As soon as I hang up, I find Janice downstairs.

"I guess we should have seen it coming," she says, closing her book. She's been waiting for me to get off the phone so we can go to bed.

"Seen what coming?" I say.

She looks at me and then rests her hand on my shoulder.

"You don't really want your father to live the rest of his life alone, do you? What would that prove?"

"How about that he'd been faithful?"

She doesn't say anything to this and I follow her back upstairs. We undress and I set the alarm.

"Just don't let Cora get you all worked up," Janice says. "You'll be exhausted in the morning."

Later, after at last falling asleep, I dream of making love to identical Taiwanese twins, but in the morning make no mention of it to Janice. She's already busily recording her own dreams in the loose-leaf binder she keeps on her night table. Recently, because things haven't been going well between us, she's especially meticulous about her entries.

After finally finishing up my degree through the extension college, I've taken a temporary position with the city's Department of Beautification. It's an election year in New Orleans and so mostly the mayor has us beautifying the more conspicuous civic landmarks. That means clipping a lot of topiary hedges and supervising two blacks, a couple of DWIs, and a Filipino. I gave up Day One trying to enforce any kind of discipline. It's enough that I get them to mow the embankments and stay inside the truck to smoke their dope.

Monday, after plugging pine seedlings all morning, we break for lunch and I spend the hour thinking about my father. After two wars he can trigger an airport security alarm from the grenade shrapnel left in one kneecap. Still, it's impossible to get a war story out of him. For twenty years my mother couldn't wheedle him into wearing his Silver Star with the oak leaf cluster. Not even on his dress uniform.

Yet sitting in the sun today, watching my charges share a joint in the back of a battered government pickup, I have to wonder how much of my father's stiff upper lip comes from a bad conscience. Had some of those metal filings lodged in his heart as well?

The following Sunday Cora calls up with the latest dispatch from the front. The day before, she'd driven in from the city to claim a few of Mom's things before the "bitch starts selling the silver."

"Turns out it was his Saturday to host the boys for poker," my sister begins.

She hadn't warned him she was coming, and I try to imagine the look on my father's face. But ever since Cora's fiery separation from Anton, he's learned to expect the unexpected.

I ask her what he'd said.

"He said he was entertaining. Did I want to come back in an hour or so?" She stops to clear her throat. Her voice is gravelly, no doubt from staying up all night with the blow-by-blow account for Darlene. "Not to worry, I told him. I knew my way around."

My sister's new business, "Save-Your-Party," films special occasions like children's birthdays and bar mitzvahs. They always come out looking a little staged to me but her customers never seem to complain. Probably because she shoots everything through a gauze-covered lens.

"So there she was in stretch pants," Cora is saying. "Ms. Rose herself. Serving little watercress sandwiches to the high rollers."

That's when she decided to make a scene.

"So I made one. I said a few things. And not in Japanese. I could see the boys wanted to take a rain check. But Ms. Butterfly just sat on the couch looking inscrutable."

Cora suddenly holds the phone away. Darlene has come in. She waits for her to pick up the other line.

"Has she gotten to the dresser part?" Darlene asks.

"I was coming to it," Cora says.

"I love this part," Darlene says.

"So, anyway, I got a trash-can liner from the kitchen. One of those big green numbers. Meanwhile, the boys are trying to settle back down to their game. But really they're just holding their cards, waiting to see what the colonel's crazy daughter's going to pull next."

"Did she tell you her nickname?" Darlene interrupts.

"Yoko," I say.

"Isn't that priceless?"

"I told them if they were *real* gamblers, they'd stick around," Cora says. "But by then even the old man was having trouble with his poker face."

Darlene urges her to get to the dresser part.

"I emptied it out in the hall," Cora says. "She had her crap in every drawer. It ticked me off."

"The boys got an eyeful," Darlene adds happily.

"You wouldn't have believed it," Cora says. "It was Frederick's of Tokyo. Talk about the Yellow Peril."

"I thought she was Vietnamese," I interrupt.

"What's the difference," Cora says.

She describes how the others started trickling out, offering their condolences to my father. But I'm having trouble concentrating anymore. It's impossible to picture my father under such circumstances. To see him standing alone in the living room, contrite and embarrassed as his friends fled the house.

Monday morning I call in sick. My allergy is acting up and we're scheduled to lay in ligustrum all along the riverfront.

"You're letting it get to you," Janice says. She hands me two antihistamines and a glass of water. "Try to look at the bright side. Your mother never knew about it. There's that."

But, as it turns out, there isn't even that. Sifting through her bag of memorabilia, Cora has come up with evidence too damning to wait for the evening rates.

"I found some letters," she begins soberly. "Love letters."

They'd tumbled out of the trash-can liner in a single neat stack bound by rubber bands.

"So take a stab at how long it's been going on," Cora says.

I carry the phone into the bathroom. Leaning close to the mirror over the sink, I stick my tongue out. It looks pasty, especially where it was sewn together.

"Houston to *Apollo*," my sister says at last.

I explain about my sinuses. "It's something in the air down here."

"I see." She's irritated that I don't seem to be taking any of this seriously enough. "That your own father's a philanderer. That doesn't mean anything to you?"

It does, of course. But what can any of us do?

"In other words, let him dance on Mom's grave." I can hear her tapping the capped front tooth I accidentally chipped with a shovel as a child. "This is doing real wonders for my work. I just finished cutting Sheldon Rubenstein's thirteenth birthday. It's supposed to be a festive occasion. It looks like a memorial service to Anne Frank."

Wednesday afternoon, I sit in the pickup truck watching Marcos (the nickname assigned him by his racist fellow workers) dig a posthole. We're at the Burden Lane turnoff to put up an exit sign. Somehow the mayor's name manages to be prominent in the phosphorescent lettering. Marcos's companions have all stepped out of the sun and into the dark shade of several pin oaks. They sit in a semicircle, their backs to the freeway, hands cupping a joint against the faint breeze. Through the love-bug-splattered windshield I consider the ragged line of pampas grass along the median. It's a shabby job of planting, but then, as Janice consoles me, it's a shabby crew did the planting.

On the seat next to me are the dozen or so letters which my father's houseguest once wrote to him using an APO address out of San Francisco. Cora bundled the lot up and sent them special overnight delivery. After arranging the envelopes in chronological order by their postmarks, I work my way through the mangled syntax and awful grammar of each hand-printed paragraph. For three years the spelling never improves. It's always "My deerest kernel." There are no indentations, scant punctuation, endless run-on sentences. And my mother is not once mentioned.

Several times, stumped by an indecipherable phrase, I call Marcos over and he holds the letter up to the sun and smiles ruefully, his fingernails rimmed with dirt.

"She say her man make her feel 'full.'" (It looks like "fool.")

When he says this it's everything for me to keep from choking him with the damp red bandana at his scrawny throat.

"She say he must come back to her if they to be 'truly'"—spelled "chewly"—"happy again."

No doubt I'm touchy but the man gets on my nerves. He seems not to care in the least that the crew ostracizes him. The others suspect he's an illegal alien and thus stealing work from their brothers. This is absurd, of course. He's the only one of the lot to cooperate and do what I ask. Unfortunately, Marcos takes my request to help with the letters as a social invitation. As soon as he finishes with the sign, he wanders back to the truck grinning.

"This happen," he says, squinting into the sun. "It's no matter. You will forget her. You can be sure."

I open the cab door and step out onto the running board.

"You got the wrong idea. They're to my father."

However, he's already nodding his head. "Well, this happen. But you forget her, no?"

I unfold my handkerchief to blow my nose. I'm building up an immunity to the antihistamines.

Marcos peers up at me. "It is nothing," he says with deep sympathy. "In the end she will mean nothing."

Back in the office I use the WATS line to dial my sister's apartment. But she's had her unlisted number changed again and the Boston operator won't give it out.

"I'm her brother," I tell the woman. "She *wants* me to have her number."

"I'm sorry, sir. There's nothing I can do."

Twenty minutes later I manage to get through to the Special

Northeast Regional Supervisor in charge of Restricted Access Calls.

"Afraid not," she says. "Company policy."

"I understand the policy," I plead, worn down finally by her irrefutable logic. "But who the hell is supposed to have her number if I don't? This is her brother, dammit."

"I'm sure it is. But we're just not allowed to take your word for it. After all, how do we know, proof positive, that you're not the one that made her go unlisted in the first place?"

"Because I'm not. It's my sister's ex-husband she doesn't want to hear from."

She's silent for a moment, the line crackling between us.

"And how do I know you're not he?"

"Because he's Romanian for one thing and has a thick accent for another." But I can't even convince myself anymore. "Just skip it, then," I say at last. "What's another broken family to South Central Bell?"

"I'm going to break a promise," Janice says dolefully. "But I don't think your mother would mind."

We're sitting up in bed.

"My mother wouldn't mind what?" I say, and lower the ice pack from my eye.

"It's just the way you've been moping around the house the last week, honey. I think you're taking your sister too seriously. You know how she is and yet you give credence to the craziest things she comes up with."

I press the heels of both hands against my eye sockets. They feel like sponges.

"So I think I should try to put the record a little straighter." She stops as if to allow me to object. When I don't she nods soberly. "Anyway, I'm not saying your mother and I were all that chummy. We weren't. But toward the end there she really didn't have anyone else to talk to. I mean, it wasn't exactly the kind of stuff she could unload on Cora."

Her hesitancy is alarming. And when she takes my hand, I know that she wants more than anything to protect me from the truth.

But more frightening still, I know she respects the truth too much to lie. It's only one of the things that make us so very different from each other.

"Don't get me wrong. I'm not saying your mother had some kind of last-second conversion. She didn't decide, after all, that she loved her son's live-in best."

Janice has taken a full-time position at the Little Folks Day Care Center. She has a natural way with children and I recognize her tone as the same one she employs at work with her little folks. Because she honors confidences, people unburden themselves with her. But my mother is another story.

"What I'm saying is that she was completely isolated from your father. She couldn't talk to him anymore. I don't think he even knew how sick she really was. Or didn't want to. I mean, she was practically crippled, wasn't she? Whenever you or Cora came up, they'd sort of put on a show for the kids' benefit. But that was all it was."

The ice pack is melting in my other hand and I set it down. "By 'kids' I take it you mean Cora and me?"

But I know that she wants only to soothe the telling. Janice is incapable of vindictiveness.

"I guess they just didn't want to hurt you."

"Well, they did a bang-up job of it. Now I can't even dial my father without going through some Oriental answering service."

Janice smiles sympathetically. "You want to talk to him, I'll call for you."

She's the sweet voice of reason and so I can't resist lashing out at her.

"You sound like some call-in psychologist. This is my mother and sister we're talking about. You remember, the ones that were so pleased to meet you?"

She takes up the ice pack and gently applies it to my swollen face. She does this, I know, because she's afraid my teary eyes embarrass me.

"All that's over with, Teddy. We're none of us the same."

* * *

The mayor has decided to make Veterans Boulevard the most beautiful thoroughfare in the state. He believes there's a vote in every azalea blossom we can get to bloom between now and November. To that end we dump several tons of fertilizer along either side of the street. Within the hour the temperature has risen into the nineties, making the manure particularly offensive to shovel. Everyone complains except Marcos, who simply wears his bandana over his mouth like a bandit but appears otherwise unaffected by the stench. His companions, meanwhile, continually threaten to bring suit through the Labor Relations Commission, whatever that is.

I pass the morning sketching some possible site designs: How to manage the drainage, the sprinklers, the lighting. The mayor's going all out. He wants fountains, brickwork, even a couple of cypress gazebos. None of my drawings will be used, of course. A local landscaping firm and major contributor to the mayor's reelection campaign will handle everything. Still, it keeps my mind off the allergy and my sister.

Cora hasn't called in weeks. She's disowned both my father and me. But Janice believes that her grudge will pass and that we'll all eventually kiss and make up. But I doubt it. We were never a kissing family.

At the stroke of noon the others drop their shovels and drive over to the Frosttop for root beers. To keep their morale up I promised earlier to let them take the truck. Marcos stays behind with me to look after the equipment. We sit in the shade of a Japanese magnolia and watch the downtown lunch traffic whisk up the boulevard to the mall. Marcos, whose real name, he tells me, is Francis, has recently separated from his wife. She ran off with some salesman of women's hairpieces. Apparently the best wigs come from the Orient, where the hair is thick, healthy, and abundant. His wife had been approached by the salesman to buy a cutting.

"He take Missie with it," Francis remarks pathetically. "She don't even write."

I offer him half of my tangerine, but instead, he slips what appears to be a small cigar from the breast pocket of his sweat-stained cotton shirt. It is, in fact, a very large joint.

"Colombia," my friend smiles, his sharp, crooked teeth as delicate as a child's. Bought, no doubt, from his companions at triple the street rate. I try to imagine what life must be like for him here in his adopted homeland. Having been cheated on and abandoned by his wife, he's daily cheated and abandoned by his fellow workers. Although it's foolish to risk a toke in broad daylight, I don't have the heart to turn him down. He's all politeness and generosity with the joint, passing it to me as if it doesn't represent half his week's earnings. But like the rest of us he's only a temporary who the city can afford to pay coolie wages.

The drug's effect is predictable, moving over me like a familiar cloud. After a fleeting garrulousness I become pompous, reflective, and finally sentimental. Francis listens without interruption. All families are alike, I advise him. They're as tenuous and imperma-nent as the smoke we are inhaling. Having lost his, he is more to be envied than pitied. Take my own family, for example. My mother's influence on us has been formative and perhaps, in the end, destructive. Her children hero-worship. But their idol turns out to be someone else and they're left with memories they can no longer trust. Francis follows none of this, of course, but smiles good-naturedly. And, in a minute, falls asleep. His companions are tardy. They take advantage of us both.

Lately, Janice quotes statistics on the frequency of divorce among couples our own age. The charts tell us, the odds are we'd come unraveled within five years. Except what could be worse, she implies, than to wind up in our declining years, married and miserable? How much better to light up the sky if only for a brief while than to peter out in perpetual orbit. My father's own case has been instructive. Who is his daughter (or even his son, for that matter) to say that he's not now happier? Can't I read between the lines of all those confiscated letters? Can't I see what's there that so irks my bitter sister? Do I really believe it a coincidence that those bound envelopes should find their way into the sack Cora hauled home? What I would fail to see is that there are no real accidents. And that my father's mistress, like all women, should never be underestimated. As I ponder this, even if hazily, a fierce possessiveness nearly overwhelms me. My mother is gone. My father a stranger. And my sister unlisted.

This morning, after I dropped Janice off at the day care, I was halfway to work before I noticed her glasses still in their case on the dashboard. She's recently gone back to wearing contacts but still can't quite make it through the whole day with them on. When I pulled into the horseshoe driveway of the Center, I saw her kneeling beside the day care's yellow van. She was consoling one of the children who had apparently already taken a dive on the concrete. The boy's pants were shredded at the knee but the wound turned out to be superficial. In a minute Janice had convinced him to rejoin his classmates and he hobbled off theatrically. All of this I watched through the pollen-dusted windshield until she turned, her quizzical smile that of my own Miss Clark a thousand years ago in a desert a thousand miles away.

The lunch traffic along North Boulevard has subsided and my companion snores peacefully beside me. I relight what's left of the joint, holding it to my pursed lips with a sharpened drafting pencil. There's just enough for a final, dizzying toke, which I draw into my lungs lustily. The shade has shifted so that my outstretched legs are no longer sheltered by the magnolia, and I move my knees up out of the sunlight. The pickup is nowhere in sight and there's nothing to do but wait. In the meantime, while my friend sleeps, I play around with my blueprints, penciling in all sorts of decorative extras at the taxpayers' expense. But, in the abstract, my plan for the boulevard's an imaginative one, I think, and even Janice agrees that it's a pity the mayor won't use it.

PACIFIC
THEATER

I'm on the phone in my father's bedroom trying to keep my voice down. Janice thought it better I come up alone.

"Just try to relax, sweetheart," she says. "Talk to him for a change."

I pick up the brass Oriental calendar from my father's dresser. It's made from an artillery shell. "The man's been in combat half his life," I say. "Guess how many war stories he ever told me."

"What about that one where he parachuted into a dump?" Janice says.

"That was only jump school. And I practically had to hound him to death just to get it." It's a two-thousand-year calendar and I set the disk on my mother's birthday. "Anyway, I was twelve then. What chance am I supposed to have now?"

"Didn't he land on an old hospital bed or something?" she says.

"He got lockjaw from the rusty springs. He only told me that because he thought it was funny."

Janice laughs. "Your father would, wouldn't he?"

"And he hasn't changed one iota."

"Well, hound him, then."

I unwrap the phone cord from my finger. "Besides, it's depressing around here. She's turned the place into Pier One, for Christ sake."

Sing, the woman my father has been living with, is part Vietnamese, part Korean.

"Think of it as a learning experience," Janice says.

It's dark in the room, and I suddenly notice something curious about my father's bed. The mattress is moving.

"You're not going to believe what I'm looking at," I say, lifting up one corner of the quilt. "They've got a water bed. What next?"

What next, as it turns out, is a six-course meal of authentic Korean cuisine. Sing has spent the afternoon in the kitchen hunched over a steaming wok. Each vegetable comes wrapped in a thin sheet of dark green seaweed. Piled atop a hot plate on the table, strips of beef simmer in soy sauce while all around me metal dishes brim with exotic concoctions.

My father, meanwhile, acts as if the feast is only the most common daily fare for him. Nor does Sing give any indication of having slaved for hours for her guest's benefit. She only smiles shyly when I deign to compliment the moist lotus roots of her parboiled *poon* dip.

Still, there's no mistaking my father's pride in the shipshapeness of his redecorated quarters.

"I'd like to propose a toast," he says after lighting the candles.

Even in his sixties my father is still a handsome man. The racquetball no doubt helps, but more than this, he seems happier than I remember him ever being with us.

"To my bride."

It isn't the pickled egg that drops my jaw, and it's a minute before I hear any more of the toast. My heart is pounding in my ears.

"We decided not to live in sin any longer," my father is saying, still holding his glass out to Sing. "It's been long enough."

Now we're both staring at the ridiculously bashful woman seated between us.

"How long?" I manage to blurt out at last. "I mean, how long ago did you get married?"

When my father confesses that it's been nearly two years, I have trouble concentrating. Even though I should have seen it coming. They weren't exactly living as brother and sister. But it's hard not to feel a little provoked. Aren't *I* the one who drove a thousand miles to get here? Where's *my* toast? Only, it isn't sympathy I see in my

father's face. Or even gratitude for his dutiful son. It's bliss.
Second-time-around bliss that has nothing, absolutely nothing to do
with me.

"Well," I offer weakly, and Sing bows her head at her new
stepson. "All the best."

I know that he doesn't intend to be callous. It's just his way. And
that my own thin skin could use a little thickening. Besides, it's
typical. My father doesn't know the meaning of brood. I'm my
mother's son.

For dessert there's a small glutinous rice cake that's filled with
bean paste. A tradition at Oriental weddings, the happy groom
remarks.

Afterward, when Sing refuses to let me help with the dishes, I
drift dumbly down the hall to the phone.

"There you have it," I break the news to Janice. "Straight from
Number One stepson."

"Honey, I've known for a while."

My ear feels like a suction cup on the receiver. "What?"

"Your father told me."

I want to take a hatpin to the water bed or at least kick over one
of the Korean goddess lamps. "Well, look who's turning inscrutable
on me."

"I didn't think you were ready yet."

She has the stereo on, which is unusual for her.

"What were you waiting for? Chinese New Year?"

"You should try to talk to her," she says coaxingly. "Really. Her
English isn't all that bad."

"I don't have anything to say to the woman. And I've got even less
to say to her husband."

"Teddy, if it's any consolation, I was surprised too. But you're his
son. It's just going to take—"

"Time. Right?"

Her breath whistles in the phone. "Well," she says wearily,
"maybe we ought to try this conversation again tomorrow."

We both listen to the stereo for a minute and then politely agree
to call it a night.

In the hall Sing has hung up several framed scrolls commemorating my father's long military career. I study the picture of him in starched khakis and pith helmet presenting a silver bowl to some generalissimo. There's a pained expression on his face. It was about the same time my mother refused to bring the rest of us over. She wasn't interested in mosquito nets and water buffalos and military compounds surrounded by nine-foot walls.

As soon as Sing sees me, she pads into the kitchen for some *hung yun char* (almond tea) and *farr shung tong* (peanut brittle). She's been playing cards with my father. Along with ballroom dancing they take courses in bridge at the community college.

"A little colder than you're used to," my father says. He pretends to study his hand.

"Much colder."

It's the first time we've been alone together, and we're both eager for Sing to come back.

"What're you fixing now?" my father calls out to her.

But she only answers in Vietnamese.

"You don't watch the calories and they start to add up," he says, tapping the deck on the folding table.

"Like everything," I say.

He gives me a fishy look and yawns. "So what do you hear from your sister? She's been laying pretty low."

"Oh, we keep in touch. She brings me up to date."

I sit down on the rattan chair and watch him go through the cable stations with the remote control.

"The numbers come on at eight," he says. "The jackpot's up to twelve million."

Sing carries a tea tray in, and I can smell the almond.

"Your father," she says. "He always play the same numbers."

"You pick any six between zero and forty," he says. "We box them for a buck."

"Once your father get four," Sing says. She sets the peanut brittle out on my mother's china. "Closest he come."

"And what'd you get for that?" I ask her.

"Eighty bucks," my father says. "About a month's worth of tickets."

Sing wags her head. "Your father like to gamble all his money away. I tell him to buy present instead."

My father checks his watch. "It gets the adrenaline going."

I think of how Cora would have said something. But my sister doesn't have much to do with us anymore. In any event, I have my own little surprise for the newlyweds. I'm heading back tomorrow.

"Peter very lucky," Sing says. Her brother works in the city. "Only one missing two times already."

My father stoops in front of the set to adjust the picture. Someone in a tuxedo is explaining how tonight's numbers will be drawn.

"In morning," Sing says to me, "Peter come to see you. He very eager to meet your father's son."

"Well . . ."

We all stop to watch a Ping-Pong ball get sucked up through a clear plastic cylinder.

"Good start," my father says as the number is turned toward the camera.

"Not us," Sing says.

We wait out the other numbers.

"Peter and Esther have a six-year-old," my father says, turning the sound off. "You won't believe the kid's English. She's always correcting her parents."

Sing is smiling proudly. "Once she stay with your father and me. She not want to come home again."

"Where'd her parents go?" I ask.

"Nowhere," my father says. "They just wanted some time to themselves. Peter's an interesting character. He taught himself computers. Three years ago he's driving a taxi in the city. Now he's pulling down twice my retirement."

Like his sister, Peter was born in Saigon, where their father had been a successful manufacturer.

"The Vietnamese businessman's worse than your Japanese," my father says. "They're nonstop. They don't know when to quit."

I ask Sing what kind of business her father had been in, but we've been talking too fast for her.

"He was back and forth to Taiwan," my father says. "Before Uncle Ho took a bead on him."

Sing doesn't stop smiling, and so it's a minute before I realize what my father has just said.

"He was shot down?" I say.

My father cups his hands like a plane nosediving. "On his way to his shoe factory."

Sing cracks a piece of peanut brittle between her teeth and blushes. It's the first time I've seen her eat anything. She can't weigh a hundred pounds.

My father gets up to peer out the window at the gray sky. "Supposed to get some snow."

"You like more tea?" Sing asks me. "Very good for hair." She smiles at my father.

It's the mother's side determines, of course, but I don't say anything.

Sing stacks our plates. She hand-washes them in the kitchen despite the automatic dishwasher.

"What's on the tube tonight?" my father asks as soon as Sing comes back with the kettle. Whenever she's out of the room we struggle to make conversation.

"Your father like his TV," Sing says. "All the time he watching the news."

"I switch around," my father says. He holds up the remote control. "You can see how they twist the same story. It's whatever they want it to come out."

I think of how my sister would have caught my eye.

"At least with Cronkite," he says, "you feel the guy has a little more to him."

Sing has fixed a darker tea for herself. She studies the guide for something that might interest my father.

"Didn't Peter Jennings adopt a Vietnamese kid?" I say. "I thought I read that somewhere."

My father only stares at the commercial.

"It wouldn't surprise me in the least," he says.

I follow Sing back into the kitchen, and she smiles expectantly at me. "I thought I'd have some Coke," I say.

She rinses a clean glass from the shelf and dries it with a paper towel.

"Your father fall asleep now," she says, twisting the cap from the liter bottle. "Sometime he feel a little sore."

"He ought to quit that ridiculous racquetball," I say, but it's more for my benefit than hers.

She sets the bottle back on the counter. Nothing in the house is allowed long out of its place. "He take his medicine," she says, rubbing her hands together as if to point out where it hurts. "Only, his fingers not change."

"His fingers?" I say. "I don't understand."

"Your father not going to say," and she giggles as if at a promise not to tell. "He just go to sleep and wake up better."

Her broken English requires a fierce concentration and I focus cross-eyed on her lips.

In the living room my father sleeps with his chin on his chest. His hands, resting peacefully on his stomach, rise and fall with his faint breathing. And for the first time I see that his thumbs are gnarled and swollen.

I tiptoe back down the hall looking for Sing. I want to ask her about tomorrow. But she isn't in the kitchen or the dining room. I don't think to knock on my father's bedroom door but as soon as I push it open, Sing, bent over at the waist, looks upside down at me, her shiny black hair nearly touching the rug.

"Christ, I'm sorry."

She's holding my mother's sterling silver hairbrush.

"You use phone," she says, apologizing for me. "Other one wake up your father."

She tries to move past me but I block the door with my arm.

"It's your house now," I say. "I should knock."

With the brush behind her back she covers her mouth with her other hand. "Your father wake up in maybe half hour."

I nod. "I'll make a quick call, then." And I lower my arm. "I'm charging them to my own number."

But she only smiles, easing the door shut after her.

Janice, pulled from her shower, nevertheless listens patiently.

"I think it's all the serenity getting to me," I tell her. "He sits around like Gautama or something. I mean, it's the Inn of the Sixth Happiness up here."

"They get along," Janice says.

"And my folks didn't," I say. "Is that what you're saying?"

"You know better than me, Teddy. You were there."

"That's right. And now I'm here. Wherever the hell that is."

"Your father's not going to change, you know. He's an old soldier and old soldiers never die. That's what you tell me all the time, isn't it?"

"You're saying he's just going to fade away."

"Teddy, honey, you might as well dig a great big foxhole and jump in. Your father's your father. He was that way with your mother. He was that way with your sister. Why should he be any different with you?"

"What about Sing?"

"I don't know," she says. "Maybe it helps not to speak the same language."

In the morning a bright white glare illuminates my bedroom like a floodlight. It's been a while since I've seen snow, and raising the bamboo shades, I wipe my sleeve across the glass. Everything is either white or black. The property slopes down steeply to the frozen lake. My mother hated the claustrophia of wherry housing and insisted on a big backyard.

On my bedstand there's a covered cup of tea and two almond cookies. I dip my finger in and it's still warm.

Sing is in the kitchen making pancakes, which incredibly she flips with chopsticks.

"Your father outside," she says.

She turns her back to me to adjust the gas on the stove. Her straight black hair is streaked with gray. Although younger than my father, she's hardly a young woman. And then I wonder how long they must have known each other. There's always been a large Asian community in the area, and I just assumed that they met here. But then I've never really gotten the chronology straight. The few times my father ever wrote or called, Sing's biography was always nebulous.

"How many for you?" Sing asks. The warming plate is stacked high with pancakes.

"A couple's fine."

She pours a tall glass of orange juice. "Your father think you too skinny. I tell him because you don't have wife."

"What's he doing out there?"

Sing wipes the kitchen window with a dish towel and taps on the glass.

"He likes to shovel it," she says.

My father signals that he's almost done.

"It runs in the family," I say.

At the garage door I watch him hike the shovel briskly over his shoulder, his breath steaming in the cold air.

"Breakfast," I shout.

But there's only a small patch to go and he raises his gloved hand without looking up.

On the other side of the car, stacked against one wall of the stucco garage, are several boxes with TROPHIES printed in Magic Marker across them. I pry open the lid on the top one and pull out a brass plaque with my father's name on it. It's for some tournament last year in Las Vegas.

"Your father not let me bring them in house," Sing says when I ask her about the boxes.

"He was really in Nevada just to play racquetball?"

"Last time to Canada. Your father senior champion."

"You're kidding."

"Have to be sixty," she says proudly. "Golden Masters. Your father win all time."

In the dining room I sit at the table until I hear my father stamping his boots on the porch. I feel like telling him that I'd forgotten to mention the lottery I won last month. Ten million a year for the rest of my life. I'm thinking how he doesn't share anything with me. Doesn't tell his own son a damn thing. He never has. And never will. By the time he sits down at the table, his ears red tipped and his face beaming robustly, I'm frustrated enough to empty my pancakes in his lap.

"I thought I'd swing by and see Cora tomorrow," I say finally, setting my knife on the edge of my plate. "Then head on back."

My father stirs his coffee. Sing has given him a large soup spoon, which he grips awkwardly.

"Sorry to hear it," he says. "We had some things planned."

"Tomorrow?" Sing asks my father. "He go home?"

"Sounds like it," he says.

"Oh, no," Sing says to me sadly.

My father folds the corners of his paper napkin into an origami stork. "You're not exactly driving a snowplow."

"I'll take it easy," I say.

But we all turn at the sound of a car in the driveway. Sing stands up and quietly lifts her chair back under the table.

"Sound like Peter," she says.

"Sounds like a damn tank," my father says.

We don't bother with our coats. Although Peter appears at least as old as his sister, his wife, Esther, looks younger than me. Their daughter, Roberta, hugs Sing about the waist.

"You'll put that thing out of alignment," my father scolds his brother-in-law.

The car, a bright red Mercedes, is laden down with chains on all four tires.

"This deep," Peter says, patting his ankle to show how much snow has fallen on the freeway.

My father looks over at me. "There you go."

Esther and Sing collect bags from the trunk of the car and carry them into the kitchen. Roberta trails after them with a Snoopy doll balanced on her shoulder. Only Sing, the first to get her green card, has yet to adopt an American name.

At the door Peter peels off his galoshes. He's dressed up: a pinstripe suit and black wingtips. And I wonder how much of this is for me.

In the living room my father turns a football game on but keeps the volume low. He's obviously heard his brother-in-law's stories before. And Peter is a talker even though his English isn't much better than Sing's.

Although the women stay in the kitchen, Sing is her usual attentive self. Every five minutes she emerges to check our glasses or to carry out another snack tray. I never hear a peep from the child.

By halftime my father is out cold on the couch. And I discover that Peter (who, innocent of any intrigue, answers all my questions candidly) has known him even longer than Sing.

"So you two go back a ways together?" I say, but rephrase it when he only smiles blankly. "You've been friends for what? Since before Roberta was born?"

"Yes, yes," he says happily. "Your father my commanding officer. All through war."

But this is typical of my closemouthed father. He'd never said anything. Never mentioned exactly when he met my step-mother. Or that it hadn't, as a matter of fact, even been in this country.

"You were with his battalion, then?" But it all makes sense, of course. My father had volunteered a second combat tour despite my mother's long-distance tirades and suspicions.

It shouldn't exactly be a revelation to me this long afterward, of course. For once I might have listened to my sister.

"Yes, yes," Peter says solemnly. "Your father very great man."

There's no point in calling Janice. I know what she'd say. My mother has been dead and buried a long time.

My father hasn't budged at the end of the couch. He looks like a crafty barn owl with his chin tucked against his chest. And I'm reminded of how he always used to fall asleep while we watched *The Big Picture* together on Saturday afternoons. It wouldn't surprise me if he asked Peter out here on purpose. But as I stare at his painfully swollen hands I can't help wishing that they were mine and not his to suffer.

Peter, meanwhile, watches with a foreigner's fascination the parade of high school bands that march with military precision across the football field. Sing, clearly happy with the miraculous assembly of her new family in one place, comes in to set a bowl of pretzels down like an offering on the table before me.

Even though I try, it's impossible to hate her. To believe she's anything more than what she is: a Vietnamese immigrant by way of Saigon by way of some idiot war by way of Boston. Safe here in America with her arthritic, racquetball-playing retired colonel and his sullen son.

I borrow my father's boots from the hall closet and sneak out of the house through the garage. The snow is already crusty on top, and in the backyard I can see where my father must have put his tomato plants in this year. The row of sticks barely pokes through the drift of snow along the basement wall. No matter where we were stationed or how little soil my father had to work with, he always seemed to have tomatoes picked and ripening on the kitchen windowsill.

Down closer to the lake I find the apple tree Sing had told me about. It's a strange-looking hybrid: its branches gnarled from various graftings. I can't quite picture the thing in bloom, but in the summer, my stepmother assures me, it will produce several different kinds of apples. She's shown my father how to band the limbs together, and next season he wants to put in a whole orchard of them.

I've decided to hang around a day or two longer. Who knows? Maybe Roberta's my half-sister. It wouldn't surprise me in the least. Yet I noticed that the six numbers on my father's lottery ticket were our birthdays, my mother's included. I would have thought he'd forgotten all that. The way only great men can. But when I turn back toward the house, I look up to see everyone smiling down at me from the big picture window of the living room. Peter is waving, his diminutive wife next to him, while at their feet their daughter presses her small, flat face to the glass. And on either side of them, like happy temple dogs, stand Sing and her bridge partner. An all-American family, I think, and struggling back up the embankment, try to keep from slipping in my father's unlaced combat boots.